A Pocketful of Stones

The Arts Council
An Chomhairle Ealaíon

First published in 1999 by
Marino Books
an imprint of Mercier Press
16 Hume Street Dublin 2
Tel: (01) 661 5299; Fax: (01) 661 8583
E.mail: books@marino.ie

Trade enquiries to CMD Distribution
55A Spruce Avenue
Stillorgan Industrial Park
Blackrock County Dublin
Tel: (01) 294 2556; Fax: (01) 294 2564
E.mail: cmd@columba.ie

© John Evans 1999

ISBN 1 86023 088 1

10 9 8 7 6 5 4 3 2 1

A CIP record for this title is available
from the British Library

Cover design by Penhouse Design

Printed in Ireland by
ColourBooks Baldoyle Dublin 13

A POCKETFUL OF STONES

JOHN EVANS

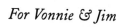

For Vonnie & Jim

BRANDON

I

My name is Brandon Marlowe. It defines me. Brandon Marlowe. I came chubby-cheeked and angry into the world seven years before Don Corleone tumbled through his tomato plants. But my mother was a fan, so that was that. The woman's ham-fisted homage defined me and condemned me. I became almost something. Like an echo. An also-ran. Askew.

Mother was a lumbering woman, lethargic and heavy-limbed. Big-boned, she used to say. She came to Ireland, twelve years old, seeking refuge with distant relatives. Flight. She arrived, mute, and stood alone beside her bag on the platform at Wexford railway station while her mother's second cousin fetched his bicycle. War raged on in Europe. She folded her coat across her arm, touching the brim of her hat for reassurance, and longed for home. Her parents, lost in Dresden, never came to claim her.

So she remained. Dislocated. Foreign. A lifetime and a language later, my father, Francis Marlowe, greatly taken with her blond hair and blue eyes, pursued her German beauty. He courted her with a zest that promised more than twenty years of marriage would deliver. One drunken night in June, long after dreams of romance had been dashed, I was conceived. He must have come all thumbs and fumbling fingers, whiskey stale, unshaven, heavy on her bed. Did she resist? I think she closed her eyes, succumbing, forgetting for a moment how the expanses of her flesh seemed to repulse him. She dared to hope that he had overcome his disappointment with the ponderousness of age. I fancy she ignored the coarseness of his hands on her and, fleetingly and wishfully, felt loved. And thence I came.

When I was ten, I watched the flesh fall from her. Her coronary thrombosis killed her slowly, her life force seeping from her with each passing pound. She was barely recognizable in the end. A skeleton. Her hair completely grey. Her life was only forty-three years long. My father came to my room to tell me she was dead. He sat on the edge of my bed and sighed. *Your mammy's gone away.* A child, I saw a softness that I never saw again. He seemed to grieve for me, not for himself. Perhaps, deep down, he was aware of his own shortcomings. Aware of how alone she had left me.

Francis Marlowe was a gravedigger but he facilitated little light relief. Once I saw him working, the year before the stroke. The year the Arklow train caught Jimmy Roche. All summer long we skipped across the train track, taunting. Sunburned shoulders, tar baking in the sleepers, we became invincible. Untouchable. Until . . .

. . . Jimmy left it late. Green grass splashed crimson, like a wave crashing. We stood in the train's thunder, squealing brakes, screaming, rooted to the bank, our faces frozen. Jimmy's arm lay disembodied beside the track, the only piece to follow us across. Summer's end.

We gathered around the grave. Class, to be seen. Knot. Herd. Teachers prodded us along until we stood shuffling, flanked by minor mourners.

'Hey Marlowe.' Murphy appeared at my left shoulder, whispering in my ear, 'What's the last thing that passed through Jimmy's mind?' He paused, waiting for me to return his smile. 'His arse.' Mr O'Driscoll clipped the boy's ear and moved him through the throng, leaving me open-mouthed, uncomprehending, struggling to understand my loss and the other boy's callousness. Forbidden humour, hidden, like a delicious secret in the dormitory at midnight. It bubbled in Murphy. Cruel. Desperation. He was in shock. We all were.

I watched my father leaning on his shovel, a stranger with a handkerchief knotted on his head. His meaty hands looked impotent, hanging limp, wrists crossed underneath his chin. Not red and scrubbed and swollen, like late at home when he would take his belt to me. Father Dunne led us in the rosary. Father cleared his throat and spit a glistening globule. *Our Father.* I was afraid of him. Until the hour of his death.

When I think about him now, I am a small boy, frightened, pausing as the teachers lead us back across the graveyard. Jimmy's body lies broken in a box beneath him. Dark stains form rings underneath his armpits, his shirt flaps open, the sleeves rolled up to the elbows. His vest is grey and stained against the vast protrusion of his abdomen. Braces stretched tight, like his sunburned face, he puts a shoulder to the wind, cups his hands, and lights a cigarette, shaking out the match before he lets it fall. He heaves a shovelful of dirt, the muscles in his forearms rolling like bags of pennies under the tough brown skin. He flings the earth into the hole, stops, removes the cigarette from his mouth, and taps it above the grave. Above my friend. *Ashes to ashes.* He sees me then, his son, squinting at him through the bright sunlight, and smiles sinisterly through the headstones. His mouth is a cavern, mirroring the open grave. His teeth must still be home beside the bed.

I have a son. He is five. Just. His hair is long and straight. Dark, almost black, like mine. I run a comb though it and rest my hand on his head, my fingers lingering, lost for a moment in the silky feel of it. I let the comb fall on the bed beside me.

'Stand back; let me look at you.' He does so, all serious expression, watching me, waiting for approval. He is perfect. He is always perfect. 'Good boy. Now go and get your schoolbag.' He twists and runs from the room, leaving me alone.

I close my eyes. His after-image is burned against my eyelids. I can see him standing, little worried face screwed up, his left hand in the pocket of his short trousers, like twins against the full-length mirror beside the door. His mouth is mine too. And his nose, poor child. But the eyes. Oh Christ! The eyes are hers.

I see long sideways looks come, sometimes, limping out from under furrowed brow, and they are her eyes staring at me. Through me. Deep brown orbs, delicate, dripping with golden fire. I can feel her moving under me again, her hands locked behind my shoulders. I can almost touch her pale skin. The softness of it, remembered, makes me ache. A tender rocking rhythm, we are two becoming one. Her lips part silently, sweet breath rising against my cheek, a single furrow bisects her smooth brow and an exquisite pain finds its way behind her beautiful brown eyes. Then I melt inside her and fall shuddering against her like a child, my tears mixing with our sweat on the swell of her breasts. It is a night like this I fill her empty belly with my seed.

'Dad?' He is shaking me, dragging me away from her. 'You'll be late. Can't be late for work.'

I open my eyes, reluctant. Back to now. 'Thank you, Einstein.' He smiles at me. Our little joke. I tell him he has a theory for everything.

I open my eyes, reluctant. Back to now. I *had* a son.

II

Will they come to his door, this other father, as they did to mine?
'We are mindful of your loss, sir. But questions must be asked.'
Will uniforms shuffle in the hallway, while an inspector perches
in the living-room with tea and fairy cakes? Will they watch his
mind disintegrate, mindful of his loss?

*

Her reasons for leaving were manifold. She could not live with a sentience as treacherous as mine. Betrayed. A fractured sanity at best. 'A baby brings beginnings,' I told her, clutching at new life between us. Our son wriggled in my arms, red-faced, struggling to cry again, his colic compounding her depression. She would not hold him. Could not.

'It doesn't fix anything,' she said, turning her face to the wall.

I had been gone again, absent for the culmination of her pregnancy. Returned too late. Black spaces stretched between my presences, unknown to me. This time her fist found me. Pummeled into prominence, I re-emerged and took my rightful place as patriarch.

'I can't live like this,' she sobbed, her face against my chest, her hand tangled in my lank hair.

'How long?'

'An hour, a day, a week. It doesn't matter.'

We sat upstairs with Gerald amid bone china and silver

the afternoon before she embarked upon her journey. Erect, face drawn, she maintained a dangerous stillness. The baby slept quietly beside her, unnamed, uncertain. Indeterminate.

'After my separation, I fled Amsterdam for this two-bedroom fleapit,' said Gerald. Golden snuff fell like damaged snow from between his nicotine-stained fingers, coming to rest on his white, starched shirt. His silver hair was slicked back and tied in a ponytail. 'A Brazilian whore to my right, an East German trumpet player to my left. Surrounded by peasants. Thank goodness for you, my children. The last bastion of civilization. Below me, propping me up, as it were.'

'Could you not go back to England, Gerald?' I asked, innocent.

'I could, dear boy. Of course.' He fingered his goatee and fixed me with a blue stare. 'But there I would be . . . normal.'

None of us are normal. Perhaps that is why we sought out this tenuous existence. My eyes found Caroline, distant on her sofa, her eyes fixed on a spot on the wall, dark hair cropped against German midsummer. Her face still bore a pregnant tan, berry brown, freckles peppered across the tangent of her nose. A trickle of sweat wound its way down the length of her neck. I longed to kiss it away.

'None of us are normal,' I said later, carrying our son downstairs.

'I suppose not.'

'Not even you, although I haven't quite figured out your madness. Unless it's staying with me.' She smiled sadly and slotted the key into the door to our apartment, avoiding my eye. 'Perhaps I'm mad enough for both of us.'

Our hallway swallowed us, family, for the last time, Caroline pinned beneath prostitutes, communist musicians, career expats; and me, her main manacle. Me, blissfully unaware.

'Is Gerald gay, do you think?' I asked, giving the baby its bottle.

'Does it matter?'

'No. It's just . . . He seems unhappy. Lonely.'

'We're all lonely, Brando.'

I shifted our son on my arm and ran a finger across his cheek. 'We have each other.'

The baby blinked at me and sucked on, fingers spread, steepled in mid air. Caroline was silent. She opened the window and sat on the arm of her chair, both arms extended across the sill, her chin resting at her elbows, a leg extended, white shoe, brown shin, blue summer skirt. She studied the hills in the distance, listening to birdsong. I cooed at my son and tilted the bottle. Upstairs, Horst began to play. Allegro. Light notes, triumphant, floated above the garden, like musical butterflies. She sighed. The music seemed at odds with her . . .

. . . After my separation, I did not flee. Not at once and not entirely. I read her letter, sitting on our bed, then buried my face in my hands and cried for an eternity. The baby started to cry in the next room.

'Oh, Caroline,' I said, 'I cannot raise a child alone.'

*

I came here as an accountant, pinstriped. A freshly married orphan. Caroline came grudgingly but seemed to understand. I held my bride's hand as we stepped into our new apartment, our new life together. 'Look, Caroline. We could really make something of this.'

I ignored the beer stains on the walls, the filthy furniture. Pockets of expatriates had passed through here before us, leaving their mark . . . *Nothing that a lick of paint won't put right* . . .

The ghosts of transient Irishmen, renowned for wild parties, vanished under white emulsion, rolled away. Often we scrubbed until midnight before falling into bed exhausted. Arms around each other we succumbed to sleep, drained, our fingers red and swollen. *Jaysus, I never would have accused that floor of being white.* Each layer removed revealed a new perspective and, like pilgrims, we stuck boldly to our task. Out with the old. Mine was a fierce determination. Sculptor, my life a lump of stone containing masterpieces undiscovered.

'This is our chance, Caroline,' I had told her as the aeroplane swooped low across the autobahn, cars rushing like electrons below us. She had smiled at my excitement and reached across to take my hand. Our chance, my father dead behind me. His turn to drool. I had watched him linger for a decade, half paralysed, a fierce determination in his eyes. Sloped and mute, his frozen face defiant, he dragged himself from day to stilted day. A man who had spent much of his adult life in graveyards, in the end he was reluctant to belong there. Worn out at last, his left side, beaten and resigned, lay down between his right side and his wife. My grandfather and I stood shoulder to shoulder by the grave, our faces as frozen as my father's had been, until Caroline, the only other mourner, broke the spell and led us both away. No tears were shed for Francis Marlowe. 'I'm free,' I had said as the aeroplane touched down in Frankfurt. 'I can't explain it, Caroline, but suddenly I'm free.'

One Sunday afternoon we stood at the centre of our new existence, fresh-cut flowers on the coffee table, our transformation complete. Caroline put her arm around my waist and rested her head on my shoulder.

'I love you, Brando.'

I twisted my head and kissed her hair, fine strands tickling my cheek. 'Love you right back, Kiddo.'

We had arrived.

*

Caroline's lips move, but I cannot hear her voice. I step outside and see myself, motionless on a chair, my face a vacant, dead-eyed void. I really should respond but I am miles away, floating now. She notices and stretches for me, features all concern. Her hand touches me through cotton-wool, remote. Like someone else's shoulder shaking. Dreaming. Her hand rises to her mouth. Panic, suddenly. And I am miles away. *It's okay, Caroline. I'm fine.* But my lips won't move. My vocal chords are frozen, congealing in my throat. She stretches over me, her fingers feeling for a pulse. Hand on my heart, she feels me breathing. She is reassured by the warmth of me. The bread knife lies discarded by the toaster. A fly climbs on to the marmalade, like Bonnington, crossing an orange glacier. I feel her hands on my face, fairy fingers, wispy, spider's web tangled in my sideburns. She backs away, troubled, biting at a thumbnail, an arm folded underneath her heavy breasts, brown against white T-shirt. All watched passively. A tableau to be taken in. Eyes still. Dead. She moves beyond my focus.

Snap. I am returned. A cold shiver runs down my spine. I blink. She is reaching for the telephone.

'Caroline?' Her name comes, pushed from me, soft, like a furtive fart through clenched cheeks.

'Oh Jesus! Oh Christ! Brando. Brando, are you okay?' She flies across the room to me, the telephone left dangling, her hair stuck to her face by fat, black tears, mascara stained. She winds her arms around my legs. 'I thought you'd had some kind of stroke.'

'No. No, I'm all right. It's okay.' My arms feel like lead, an effort to raise a hand and put it softly on her head, her tears seeping through my jeans, wetting my knees.

'Christ, Brando, what was that? What's wrong with you?'

'I . . . I don't know.'

'You scared the living shite out of me, love.' She begins to regain her composure, sitting back on her heels now, wiping at tears with the palm of her hand, fingers splayed, long, painted fingernails and gold rings. 'Are you sure that you're all right?'

'Yeah. I'm fine. Really.'

'I'm going to call a doctor, Brando.'

'No. It's okay. It's over now.'

'How can you be sure?'

'It's happened before. When I was a child I used to have these . . . absences. Like being in a tunnel. Dark. Scary. It hasn't happened in years. It's a one-off. Probably the heat or something. Or stress. Maybe I've been working too hard . . .'

How can I convince her if I can't convince myself? My heart is beating like a jackhammer, my breathing shallow and nervous. *Christ.* Images of childhood come unbidden, drooling at the kitchen table, lost. Parents pulling me to my senses, Father shaking me, my mother's arms around my head, her viscous tears shattering slowly on my skull, until I re-emerge, small and frightened. Little-boy-lost, regained.

'I don't like the sound of this, love. There must be something we can do. Tests . . .'

'No. No tests. I've done them all before. Doctors poke and prod and guess . . . I'm not crazy, Caroline. You must believe me.'

I have surprised her, aroused her from the torpor that has threatened us for months. Now we have a common enemy. No more fights at twilight and slamming doors. *I hate it here. How can I learn this bloody language?* Sleeping separately, we make up in the mornings. *It's boredom, love. That's all. It'll be better when you have a job.* She sobs on. *But the language is so difficult. Inter-Cert German never prepared*

18

me for this. But Mother made it easy for me. *It's okay, Brandon.* Spoken in her language, beyond my last attack. *There is nothing wrong with you. Come on, we'll say a prayer.* Now Caroline will fight this with me too.

*

I came home from work for the last time to find her painting the walls in the spare bedroom. *Blue. I think that it will be a boy.* Her stomach, swollen underneath her overalls, was filled with possibility. White paint, from the finished ceiling, had speckled her expectancy, like a bird's egg. She perched on a footstool, stretching for a high corner. There were streaks of blue and white across her forehead where she had wiped away the morning's perspiration.

'Caroline, we need to talk,' I said, my briefcase in my hand, the cardboard boxes abandoned on the landing.

'Look, Brando, I'm sorry about last night. Okay? I know that I should be more understanding. It's not your fault.' A sheet lay draped across the cot that waited for our unborn child.

'Take a break, Caroline. Please.'

She paused, worried now, and stepped down from her footstool. 'Okay.' She laid her brush carefully across a paint tin and came to the door to meet me, slipping out of her mottled shoes at the edge of the newspaper strewn on the floor. She wasn't wearing any socks and I could not take my eyes off her tapered ankles, the smoothness of her shins beneath the rolled-up denim. 'Brando, are you all right? Is something wrong?'

I felt my chin tremble and closed my eyes. 'Caroline, I . . . '

Hard words from the previous night floated into my conscious-

ness. Returned, I bent beneath her anger, strong emotions crashing over me. 'I can't be alone, Brando. How much more of this do you think I can take?' She sat on the arm of the sofa, curled, bare feet twisted in the cushions, her knees pulled up against her chest. 'I'm twenty-eight years old, for Christ's sake. What kind of life is this? I need friends, a social life.'

'We have friends . . . Gerald . . .'

'Gerald is an old man, Brando. Sixty something. He's not a friend. He's an acquaintance. Christ. I can't even talk to you.'

She stood up and stormed from the room, slamming our bedroom door behind her. That night I slept on the couch, a blanket wrapped around me, and in the morning I scraped four days' stubble from my face and returned to work, my first appearance of the week. On Friday.

I stood, weak, in the hall and told her. 'They've let me go, Caroline. I've lost my job.'

She waited for the punchline, speechless, her mouth dropped open, a hand resting on her pregnancy. Her painted face mocked her, a tragic clown in stained overalls. 'They can't,' she said at last, her voice small. 'We have a baby on the way.'

'They can, Caroline. They have. Robert was sorry but he says he can't cover for me anymore. Enough is enough, I guess.'

'Oh Christ, Brando. What are we going to do?' She sank down against the wall and sat on the floor. 'What the fuck are we going to do?'

I sat beside her and took her hand. 'Look, Caroline, there's nothing to worry about right now,' I said. 'The German system will look after me for the time being. Robert was fair about it. He didn't fire me; he called it redundancy. That means I'll get full benefits for a while. But . . . I need to see a doctor. It's time. And I need you to help me, love.

Will you?'

But Caroline pulled her hand away from mine, folded her arms across her knees, and buried her head in her forearms. It was her turn to withdraw.

Later, she comes to me, repentant. 'I'm sorry, Brando. I was selfish. Are you okay?' She has bathed, cleansed herself. Her skin feels soft and warm when she puts her arms around me from behind. 'We'll be okay, love. We'll manage. We just have to get you well.' I feel warm, wet kisses on my neck and cheek. 'Forgive me.'

I twist towards her, smiling, and slip my arm around her waist. 'For what? There's nothing to forgive.'

'I love you, Brando.' She puts her hands on my cheeks, fingertips brushing my temples. The roundness of her stomach feels tight and firm against me. Worried, wrinkled forehead, she searches my face. 'That's enough, isn't it? That has to be enough.'

*

Three months later she was gone, leaving me alone to raise our son. Her post-natal depression proved too much for our struggling relationship. I took her clothes from the wardrobe and spread them on our bed, maternity dresses and winter woollens, left behind in her eagerness to distance herself from me. I imagined her, choosing, standing in her underwear after a shower, her hair dripping, water beaded on her shoulders. The child watched me from his carrycot, cooing occasionally, as if to remind me of his presence. I held a cardigan to my face and breathed in her perfume, a trace of her still resident. Her book lay open on the bedside table with its spine broken. I wondered if she missed it, sitting on a bus somewhere, realising that she would never know the outcome now.

I lifted the boy and held him in front of me. His mouth opened into a toothless grin and he stretched out a fat arm to touch my nose with his pink fingers. I carried him across the room and put him on the bed. He kicked his feet and gurgled, sprawled helpless on his back. I lay beside him amongst her scattered clothes and watched him for a long time as he stared, fascinated, at a fly crawling on the ceiling. Each of us had different thoughts to occupy us.

*

I tell him about his mother when he is close to sleep, his thumb buried deep in his mouth, loose fingers curled around his nose. I talk about her patient softness, the fine network of wrinkles at her eyes when she laughs. His head rests on my stomach, his eyes are heavy, sore from the day's spent warmth. I run my fingers through his dark curls and speak about her coming home, her hair shorn, crying because of the unexpected pregnancy, and me going to her.

'It's all right,' I say. 'Everything will work out grand.'

She lifts her face to me. 'I know.' And I realise the tears are tears of joy. 'I know.'

She holds my hand to her stomach, asking if I can feel him, and I do believe I can. Impossible, I know. A few weeks gone, it can't be more. But I feel him, the profoundness of him, and I know that our lives will never be the same.

Caroline finds us sleeping in the living-room, our son with his head on my stomach. I wake to find her watching us, her head tilted, a smile, distant, lighting her face. She sees my eyes open and raises a finger to her lips, nodding towards the child.

'I called him Donal,' I say softly. 'Is that all right with you?'

She nods and mouths his name. Donal. She moves across the room and kneels beside us, brushing his face with the tips of her fingers. Her eyes, fixed on him, widen with each breath he takes, until she turns to me, her face radiant, and grips my hand.

'I love you, Caroline,' I whisper above the boy's breathing. 'I have missed you so.'

'I know,' she says. 'I love you too. Both of you.'

But when I awake we are cold on the living-room floor. Alone, I lift my son and carry him to bed.

*

I wake, diagonal, feet failing to find her, or sit cross-legged on the floor, a pair of her starched pyjamas, freshly plucked from the hot press, folded against my cheek. My woman has deserted me.

*

'I'm calling him Donal, I'd like you to be the godfather,' I told Gerald, who laughed and slapped his thigh. 'What?' I was mystified. Gerald was stealing my thunder. I had come all formal, with a proposal – of sorts.

'A wonderful idea, Brandon. Wonderful.'

'What are you on about, Gerald?'

'Never mind. Give him here.' He took my son beneath the arms and held him in front of his face, both of them gurgling like imbeciles. 'Isn't this cosy?' he said. Don, *Brando* and the godfather. A certain symmetry, wouldn't you say?'

I smiled, realising. I had not meant to perpetuate the idolatry. 'Donal is my grandfather's name,' I said.

'Donal it is then.' He held the child aloft once more and kissed him on the forehead. 'At last, young man, a name. You have been claimed.'

'You'll be the godfather, then?'

He settled Donal on his knee and placed a hand on top of mine, suddenly solemn. 'I'd be delighted, Brandon. Honoured.'

'Thank you, Gerald. It means a lot. It's just . . . I need someone that I can count on.'

'You know that you can count on me, dear boy.' He smiled and squeezed my hand.

'No. I mean really . . . Someone who . . .'

Gerald squeezed my hand again and released it, ignoring the tears that had welled up in my eyes. He handed Donal to me. 'Hold on, Brandon. I'll get us a couple of G&Ts. Then we can have a proper chinwag.'

When he returned, Donal was lying on his back on the floor, in the middle of his blanket, examining his toes. He stepped around the child and handed me a tall glass. 'Ice and lemon,' he said. 'I took the liberty.'

'Cheers.'

He settled on the couch beside me, crossing his legs. 'Talk to me, Brandon. Now that we're raising a child together there must be no secrets.'

'It isn't easy, Gerald.' I hesitated, rubbing the back of my hand across my eyes. 'Christ, it isn't fucking easy.' I reached down and put a hand on my son's stomach, comforted by the warm softness. 'I'm frightened. I don't know if I can look after him.'

'There are lots of single parents, Brandon. You'll manage.'

'It's not that. I . . . Gerald, there are things about me that you don't know.'

'Maybe I know more than you think, dear boy.'

I looked at him sharply. 'What do you mean?'

'I know about your illness, Brandon. Caroline and I were really rather close. She needed somebody to talk to. Coffee mornings. You know, just between the girls.'

'You know?'

'I've known for quite some time.'

We sat in silence, watching the child twisting on his

24

blanket. I felt at once embarrassed and relieved, exposed but knowing that he would not mock me. He understood the nature of my torment, my struggle with myself. Father confessor, he counselled Caroline through her confusion, became her confidant, became her friend. He was there for her when I became withdrawn, patting her hand and comforting her.

'I didn't know how to tell you,' I said.

'Now you don't have to.'

'It's not as if . . . Look, Gerald, I can function normally most of the time. It's just . . . Sometimes I sort of trip-out. Like a light goes out in my head. I can't explain it.'

'Have you tried to get help?' He peered at me intently, his silver eyebrows locked together in concern.

'Doctors *can't* help. They give me different drugs, experiment. I don't want to be their guinea pig, Gerald. I want to be here for my son. Can you understand that? That's why I'm asking for your help. I need you to watch me. To . . . I can't do this alone. I need . . .' My words dribbled to a standstill. Gerald cleared his throat and stared at the floor. After a moment he looked at me above his glasses.

'For what it's worth, I told her not to go.' His voice was soft, apologetic.

'She spoke to you about it?' It was as if he had slapped me. I felt my skin tighten, blood rushing to my face. I pictured them, plotting. Huddled together on his couch. Perhaps she borrowed a suitcase from him or stored her baggage in his spare room, preparing for flight.

'Yes.' He watched me carefully, unsure of how I would react.

'Why didn't you tell me?' I spoke evenly, not wanting to betray the depth of my emotions.

'It wasn't my place, Brandon. You know that.' He

squirmed, uncomfortable. I realised that he had been dreading this conversation, knowing that it was coming. He had been bound by a code of silence, a sacred oath. 'Caroline made me promise not to say.'

'She's coming back.'

'I don't think so, Brandon.' His voice was soft, gentle. He put his hand on mine again. 'It's hard to leave a child. It isn't something done lightly. She isn't coming back. You'll have to face that.'

'She's coming back.' I spit the words again, determined. Trying to convince him. Trying to convince myself.

He patted my hand, much as he must have patted hers. 'Whatever. Never mind.' He straightened and smiled broadly. 'We'll muddle through,' he boomed. 'Won't we Donal?' Donal laughed and wriggled at his feet. Assent. 'How could we go wrong? An infant, a psychotic and a fairy godfather. How could we possibly go wrong?'

*

Before breakfast, Gerald comes knocking, bearing eggs. 'I thought you'd like an omelette,' he says in the hallway, resplendent in an emerald satin dressing gown.

'That's good of you. Come in.'

I step back and motion towards the kitchen. Donal sits in his high chair, brandishing a spoon and smiling a welcome. Gerald bends to pinch his cheek. 'He's the spitting image of his mother, isn't he?' All smiles, he puts the egg carton on the table, catches Donal's hands in his and starts to clap them. Donal laughs and starts to jig up and down, his smile widening.

'Aye. That he is.' I fall silent, watching Gerald fuss over my son, cutchy-cooing, trying not to be too obvious. 'It's okay, Gerald. I know what you're at. Ask what you want.'

Gerald freezes, a finger aimed at my son's midriff, and looks at me. The child reaches out and clasps the extended finger in his tiny hand, gurgling. Gerald opens his mouth. Then, thinking better of it, he closes it again.

'Thanks for checking, Gerald, but he's in no way mistreated. And I feed him well, in case you're worried. He'll be on to solids soon.' I smile, taking the sting out of my words, not wanting to offend him. 'Relax, Gerald. I did say I wanted someone to depend on. You're just doing your job. I appreciate it.'

He smiles nervously. 'I'm sorry, Brandon. If I transgressed . . .'

'No, Gerald. It's perfectly okay. I need you to watch me. I'm a novice at this. I can use all the help I can get.'

'I feel a proper toad.'

'You shouldn't. Sit down. I'll make that omelette.'

Over breakfast he asks me how I'm doing.

'Fine, Gerald. I'm getting over it. Getting on with my life. And then there's Donal to worry about.'

'And financially?'

'It could be worse.'

Gerald looks uneasy, another reason for his visit. 'I've been thinking about it, Brandon. I know that you haven't worked steadily for quite some time. It can't be easy. I mean, with a child and everything . . .'

'I was an accountant, Gerald. I have some money put by. Not much, but it's enough. Caroline took nothing.' I pushed the egg absent-mindedly around the plate with my fork. 'Then there's the dole. It's good here, you know. Better than in Ireland.'

'I want to help.' He interrupts, blurting the words out. He is all earnest-eyed and well-meaning.

'Thanks, Gerald,' I say with a smile, 'but it's okay. We're grand. We can manage. I appreciate it, but we don't need . . .'

'No, no.' He raises his hands, palms extended towards me, his face angled to the floor, shaking his head. I can see a bald patch on the crown of his head, camouflaged where he has combed long, silver strands across it. 'You have to hear me out. I know you won't take money from me, dear boy, so here's the deal. We'll pool resources. That's what I'm suggesting. Nothing drastic. After all, living with me would not improve your prospects as a ladies' man. Besides, I like my privacy. I've gotten used to being on my own. But you can do the washing and the ironing, a little light housework, and, in return, I'll buy all the groceries. Fair's fair. Is it a deal?'

'It's very generous, Gerald. But . . .'

'It's for my godson, Brandon.' He leans across the table and grasps my hand, his eyes searching my face, his expression one of desperation. 'You have to let me do this. You must accept.'

I feel awkward now. As if, by refusing, I will offend him, end our growing friendship. 'I'll think about it, Gerald. Okay?' 'Well, don't think for too long.' He smiles, releasing my hand and leaning back in his chair. He retrieves his snuffbox from his dressing-gown pocket and opens it. 'I let my *Putzfrau* go yesterday.' He pauses, a pinch of snuff halfway to his nostril, as if realising the enormity of his decision. 'My God. The apartment will fall to pieces if the cleaning's left to me.'

I laugh at the mock horror on his face. 'I guess we have a deal then. We can't have you living in squalor.'

'Indeed not, dear boy. Indeed not.' He snorts the snuff and sneezes noisily, causing Donal to jump in his highchair.

*

We are thrown together, tortured souls. I lie awake in bed sometimes and hear Gerald moan and wake above me. He was always there, unheard. But she lay between us, like soundproofing. I can hear his feet thumping on the carpet as he climbs out of bed. My ceiling creaks beneath his weight. He stands, and wanders towards the kitchen. I think of him, hunched over his whiskey glass, his eyes rubbed red from lack of sleep and lonely tears. Tomorrow he will greet me and take Donal in his arms, all smiles and corpulence, like Santa Claus. Donal may tug at his goatee. He will wear his silver hair tied back as always, held with an elastic band, the skin around his blue eyes, tired behind wire-rimmed glasses, looking stretched, almost Chinese. And he will take his snuffbox from his shirt pocket and snort a pinch, deep, until his eyes water.

I love this man. The depth of him. His courage and his strength. 'I'm just an old queen,' he cries one night, theatrical, drunk in his living-room again. 'Isn't that horrid. All these years and here I am, alone. Nothing but an old queen.'

'You're not alone, Gerald,' I tell him, putting an arm around his shoulders. 'You have us. Me and Donal.'

But the man still sobs, lamenting a lifetime spent avoiding confrontation. 'My father just could not accept it,' he recalls, 'No son of mine, he used to say. England in the forties. No son of mine. Christ, Brandon. I thought that there was something wrong with me. Some sort of disease. A vile infection. And when I tried to talk to Mother, she just didn't want to know. Oh Brandon, I have been running all my life.'

'We're all running, Gerald. It's just that we all run for different reasons.'

'But my reason was taboo. A filthy secret, Brandon. Shameful. Dirty. I moved to Amsterdam in 1953. It seemed the place for me. Obscenity everywhere. The perfect place to hide my dire depravity. I wallowed in the mire with other queens and miscreants. Began my double life. By day I was a self-respecting member of the wunch.'

'What's the wunch, Gerald?'

'It's the collective term for bankers, boy.' He giggles for a moment, pleased to have caught me, but the pleasure passes from his face as suddenly as it had appeared. His chin drops, leaving a dark hole in his features, his lips red and moist against the whiteness of his teeth and the paleness of his skin. 'You have no idea, Brandon,' he says, as if the enormity of his life-decision is occurring to him for the first time, 'no idea what it's like.'

'Maybe not, Gerald. But I'll tell you one thing, though. You're wrong. You're not just an old queen.'

'No?' He looks at me, all shiny-eyed.

'No. You're a drunk as well.'

And with that he splutters and snorts and collapses against me, convulsing with laughter.

'Now go and get us another drink, you moany old fucker,' I say, pushing him towards the door.

*

Donal is a good child, a credit   to me. He is not prone to tantrums, but stands silently in his cot mornings waiting patiently and beaming when I come to retrieve him. It is easier than I anticipated to raise a child alone, but then, I am not alone. Gerald dotes on the boy, the son that he will never have. He would spoil him if I allowed it. Would spoil me too. There is a tenderness about him that is rare, as if his extravagance is all an act, calculated, invented to protect him. Sometimes I catch him with his guard down, watching

Donal maybe, his face soft and open. Or, when I find myself slipping, he will recognise the change in me and offer to take my son to stay at his place. *Come and get him when you're ready, Brandon.* I floated back to cognisance once to find him feeding me soup. He sat with a spoon hovering, as if feeding a child, concern written all across his features. He made light of it, avoiding my eye, uncomfortable for me, clearing his throat and staring at his slippers.

And all the time Donal grows quietly, stretching out of baby clothes. I record his evolution, a diary and photographs, keepsakes for Caroline. She misses his first tooth, his first step, his first word. Instead I share them with Gerald. Donal totters towards us on a rainy afternoon in spring, saliva swinging from his mouth, intent on making the transition in his bright red corduroy overalls. I stretch my arms out, waving him home, and Gerald, kneeling beside me, claps his hands and whoops in delight. When he lurches into my arms, I hug my son, laughing with him, Gerald's hands resting on us, and suddenly it is as if a hole appears in my chest, a great gaping void. My hunger for her takes on new dimensions. Empty, I clutch what I have left of her to me, feeling him kicking at my thighs as the tears come.

Gerald stands over me one night, holding my face in his hands and squeezing at my temples, trying to force me to see sense. 'You have to let her go, God damn it, Brandon.' His voice is hard, cruel to be kind. His eyes pierce me, a fierce intensity. 'You must live your life. For Donal if not for yourself.' I snivel in the half-dark and bite my tongue, salt blood welling inside my mouth. He releases me, sighs and leans against the wall beside the door. 'I wish I had your youth, Brandon. You have no idea.' The fight is gone from him. 'I wish that I could make you see . . . She's gone, my boy. You have to face that.'

31

'No.'

'Brandon,' he kneels in front of me, pleading, 'Please. You can't keep doing this to yourself. I shan't let you.'

When he leaves I open Donal's bedroom door. A triangle of light from the hallway falls across his cot. He is draped in sleep, his small body curled around itself, foetal, undulating softly. She carried him for me and now it's my turn. I will keep him safe and warm, present him to her, perfect, when she chooses to return. Tomorrow he will wake before me and stand waiting, hands wrapped around the bars, like a happy prisoner. And when I come for him he will jig up and down, his red-cheeked, damp-chinned smile welcoming me. I will lift him, reassured by the healthy solidness of him, and we will start another day. Over breakfast we will grin at each other like we always do. The men. Then, as he sucks his toast into submission, I will catch a shadow of her in him and my breath will stick in my throat. She has not left me entirely. I know that I am bound to see more traces. Tomorrow.

III

My madness is stretching, becoming more pronounced. The darknesses last longer now, thinning, punctuated and populated by shadows. Reality intrudes, lumbering, like whales moaning. Merging. Sometimes it is hard to see the joins.

*

I lost another job last week. Unemployed. Again. If it wasn't for Gerald . . . *Caroline is coming back.* The thought comes arcing like a lifeline sometimes. All I have to cling to. *She just has to find her way.*

Donal is two today. Gerald prepared the party. He mothers both of us, God bless him. Horst and Rita come, dressed for work. She leaves at six, stilettos staccato on the stairs. Horst has an engagement. He stands nervously in the corner of Gerald's kitchen in a dress suit, his trumpet-case clutched under his arm, like a Mafioso just before a hit.

'*Prost!*' Gerald toasts us and helps Donal blow out the candles. All two of them. We tear the paper off his presents with him. What I could afford. And Gerald's generosity, a trampoline. 'Something for Daddy,' he says, handing me a bottle. We drink, poured into chairs, while Donal bounces.

'We belong here, you and me,' says Gerald. 'Where else would we survive? Sad creatures, aren't we?'

'Aye. Sad.' The whiskey burns my throat, makes me numb. We sit like this, watching, until Donal succumbs to sleep, bounced out, then carry him together to the guest-room and place him between the sheets. My son. Our child. His as much as mine.

Gerald leans towards me and whispers across Donal's soft breathing. 'I have another bottle.'

I raise an eyebrow. 'Lead on.'

Inebriation finds a foothold and climbs aboard. Refuge from the demons. We sprawl, reluctant to return.

'It's like this,' I tell him, trying to explain my affliction. 'Like I'm drunk. A kind of otherworldliness. A vanishing of sorts. That's what it is. And dark when I return. Forgotten.'

'Like an alcoholic. *Lost Weekend*. Remember Ray Milland?'

'Kind of. But . . . not. I can't describe it, Gerald. It's not as if I bring it on myself. I can't predict it. It just . . . happens.'

'Like shit.' And he collapses into near hysterical laughter. I smile across the room at him. Infectious.

'I've got to go, Gerald. I'm bolloxed. Thank you for tonight.'

'My pleasure, dear boy. My pleasure.' He stands and extends a hand, which I shake. 'And what about the tike?'

'We'll not disturb him. I'll collect him in the morning, if that's okay.' Gerald nods and leads me to the door. 'Goodnight, Gerald. Thanks.'

'Goodnight,' he whispers and closes the door softly behind me.

I find myself outside Rita's door, knocking quietly. She answers, opening the door a crack. I fumble in my pocket, pull out a few crumpled banknotes and proffer them. 'It's all I have.'

She opens the door wider and beckons me inside, her terrycloth robe falling open, exposing large nipples, like dark secrets atop small, brown breasts.

'Put away your money,' she says quietly as I step across her threshold.

*

When I come, I breathe a name. Caroline. Rita puts her arms around me and holds me, her body small and hard beneath me, patient. I bury my face in her hair and weep quietly. For Caroline. For Donal. For me. I feel myself shrink inside her and she rolls from under me, pushing me aside. She stands beside the bed, her back to me, and pulls her robe around her shoulders; then flicks the long black ringlets of her hair from underneath the collar with her hand. Her fingers are long and slender, like a pianist's. Delicate.

'Wait.' She holds a hand in front of me, pink palm like a scar against the darkness of her skin. I turn on to my back and pull her sheet around me.

When she comes back she is carrying two mugs of steaming coffee. She hands one to me, folds a leg and settles on the edge of the bed.

'Where is your son?'

'With Gerald. Asleep. I didn't want to wake him.'

She sips her coffee, both hands wrapped around the mug, regarding me above the rim. Deep brown pupils, soft, swim in startling white either side of the handle.

'I'm sorry,' I say, blurting, suddenly ashamed.

'For what?' Her voice is neutral, calm, her eyes fixed unblinkingly on mine.

'For coming here. For expecting . . . I . . .' But thoughts slip wordlessly away and I am left afloat on her bed, inadequate.

'It's okay. I know you're lonely. I've watched you with the boy.' She shifts, drawing both legs under her and settling the mug in her lap. She puts an elbow on the bedstead and rests her head on her hand.

My eyes drop to the bedspread, crumpled on the end of the bed, to my fingers playing with the mug, sliding on the hot ceramic. 'I should not have said her name.'

'Men say things,' she says, shrugging, and I feel heat rise to my face, embarrassed by her profession. By the need for it. By *my* need for it. 'You miss your wife.' A simple statement, obvious. As if she understands my pain and elects to expose it as mundane melancholy. Her words casually dismiss my torment, de-dramatize my torpor.

'Yes, I miss my wife.' Eventual admission.

'We are all lonely.' Cold sting.

'She said that, the night before she left. I didn't realise how lonely she was, how unhappy she must have been.'

'She should have told you.'

'Perhaps she did. Perhaps I wasn't listening.'

She breathes beside me. Slow, measured inhalations. Waiting. Nothing to say, she says nothing. But she is here. A calm presence, comforting. There is a safeness in her room. It is a sacristy of sorts, her clothes scattered, jeans juxtaposed with epicurean extravagance. My eyes find hers. I see her, as if for the first time. I had not noticed how young she was. A child. A beautiful child.

'Thank you for your kindness,' I say, feeling suddenly tired again, my eyes heavy, closing. She leans across and kisses me gently on the eyelids, a hand resting, feather-soft, on my chest.

'Go home now,' she whispers.

*

Horst stopped me in the corridor a few days later, his door opening as I carried Donal towards Gerald's apartment. He barred my way, his smile a nervous tick pulling at the corner of his mouth, his left hand held behind his back.

'I . . .' He hesitated, words eluding him.

'What can I do for you, Horst?' I smiled at him,

36

hoisting Donal on my hip.

'Thank you for the party,' he muttered, quickly, before his courage deserted him, his eyes fixed on a point on the wall beside my left shoulder. He pushed something into my hand. 'For the boy,' he said, and then retreated hastily, his door closing noiselessly. His present was a perfect, six-inch pony, carved carefully from a single block of wood. I handed it to Donal, who put it in his mouth.

'There you go, kid,' I said. 'The start of the farm.'

'Horse,' he said, grinning at me.

Gerald was watching, amused, from his doorway. 'I do believe that Horst is becoming an extrovert,' he said.

'What?'

'Well, after all, he looked at *your* shoes when he spoke to you.'

*

I am at her door again, this time bearing flowers. Inside, she rattles chains, prepared to lower her defences. She emerges, a towel wrapped around wet hair, wearing jeans and a T-shirt.

'Hi,' I say, the flowers held behind my back. 'I . . . Well I . . .'

'Yes?' She raises an eyebrow and bends her head to see what I am concealing.

'Here.' I hold the flowers out to her, twelve red roses. 'For you.'

'Thank you,' she says, 'it's sweet.'

We stand there for a moment, tension building between us. My hands feel awkward, now that they are empty, so I put them in my pockets. I smile at her, embarrassed. 'I just wanted . . . Rita, thank you for the other night. For being there. I just . . . Sorry, I'm not very good at this.'

'At what?' She bends her head and breathes the perfume from the roses.

'I don't know, but whatever it is I'm not very good at it.' There is silence again. She looks amused. I take my hands out of my pockets and shrug, my palms turning towards her, a smile touching my lips again. 'Help?'

'Dating? Is that what this is?' She smiles.

'Maybe. I'm afraid I'm a little out of practice.'

'Well, would you like a coffee?'

'Yes. I would like that very much.'

She steps aside and motions me into her apartment. Her kitchen is neat and well-appointed. She drapes the towel across a chair and her dark hair falls in wet curls around her, leaving wet stains at the collar of her T-shirt. The coffee is already brewed. It stews quietly beside the microwave. It is the first of her habits that I come to recognise, always have a coffee standing by.

'Brazilian,' I say, as she hands me the cup. She smiles, nodding, returns to the worktop and begins to snip the stems from the roses. I sit, with my elbows on the table, watching her. 'I'm sorry about the other night,' I say to her back.

'Really?' She makes a half-turn towards me, the scissors dripping in her hand, an eyebrow arched.

'That's not what I mean . . . I'd just like if we could start again.'

She arranges the flowers in a vase and places it on the window sill, then pours herself a cup of coffee.

'Rita, I don't want you to think that . . .' I look away from her, ashamed of myself. She walks across the room to me and puts a hand on my shoulder.

'It's all right. I think I understand.'

'No,' I say, putting my hand on hers and looking into her eyes, 'it's not all right. I've lived in this house for four years with you and Horst and I realised the other night that I don't know either one of you. We pass in the corridor; we say hello and smile. Then, after a time, there is only awkwardness between us. We still smile, open doors for one another, but the opportunity for more than that has passed. On special occasions, like Donal's birthday party, we inhabit separate corners of a room. Together, but not. We should know each other better, but we don't. We've been neighbours for a long time. Perhaps we should be friends. Who are you, Rita? I don't know who you are.'

'I am an *Ausländer*, Brandon. A foreigner, like you. Faceless. Here, that is all that any of us are.' She pulls away from me and moves around the table to another chair, sitting gracefully. Her coffee cup rests between her hands, palms flat on the table. 'Even Horst. German, but foreign. East German, different. We pass each other in corridors because we are displaced, because we are damaged. Our solitude is our sanctuary.'

'Is it?'

'We are all running, Brandon. It's not unusual.'

I suck my lower lip and look at her, unsure of what to say.

'Do you want to be friends, Brandon?' she asks.

'Yes,' I say. 'Very much.'

'Okay. Then let's be friends.'

'As easy as that?'

'As easy as that.' She sips her coffee, lifting the cup with both hands, like an offering. 'I remember your wife,' she says after a moment. 'She was very beautiful.'

'Yes. She was.'

'Did you love her very much?"

'Yes.'

'Good. Then you are lucky. You have known love.' She drains the coffee from her cup and stands up. 'More coffee.' It doesn't seem to be a question.

*

She took us to Mass on Sunday morning, insisting. Lapsed, I allowed her to lead me to a pew, Donal in my arms. The smell of the church reminded me of childhood, a mixture of must, incense and furniture polish. I thought of Sunday mornings with my mother, dressing quietly, afraid to wake my father; his snores, muffled through the wall, a testament to Saturday's over-indulgence. Spick and span, I held her hand and walked down Waterloo Road to the Friary and ten o'clock Mass. I remembered the solemn silence, the coolness of the church's interior, the reassurance of her hand wrapped around mine, the sense of belonging radiating from her, her heels clicking on the flagstones. A generation later I sat beside my son, finding comfort in the familiar propriety of the ceremony.

Rita reached for my hand and squeezed it. I turned to her and found her smiling at me across my son's head. She remained insistent at communion time, pushing me ahead of her into the aisle. Fingers trembling, the priest placed the host on my tongue and I felt myself shiver as the wafer began to dissolve in my saliva. I remembered, as a child, holding the host to a toothache, believing that God was truly in my mouth and knowing that the pain would dissipate. I mourned the loss of that blind faith, the certainty that everything would turn out as it should.

Donal, feeling left out, made his presence known. 'Papa, Papa. Brot essen. Brot.' The priest grinned and put his hand gently on Donal's head before we moved away. Rita and I walked down the aisle together, smiling, Donal, his legs forced apart by Pampers, swinging between us like a mutant chimpanzee.

Outside, we squinted in the sunlight and allowed Donal

to balance on a wall like a tightrope walker. He swayed between us, concentrating on his feet, unconsciously tightening his grip on our hands.

'Doesn't it seem strange?' I asked.

She looked at me, confused. 'What do you mean?'

'Well . . . It's not what you'd expect. I mean, given what you do for a living. I'm sorry. It's just that . . . Don't you think that what you do is . . . sinful?'

'Don't judge me, Brandon,' she said evenly, no trace of anger in her voice. 'It is between me and my God.'

I watched her monitoring Donal's progress, her left arm held up, holding his small hand in hers, her right arm shooting out instinctively to help him regain his balance after every faltering footstep. Together we kept him from falling.

'Thank you, Rita,' I said.

She looked up at me. 'For what?'

'For bringing us here. For helping us find another kind of sanctuary.'

She smiled. 'You're welcome.'

*

She anchors me. Strange. Hers is a solid sadness. Alone, we skirt around the edge of our existence, uncomfortable observers. Together we become a kernel, feeding off each other.

I am stronger than I have ever been. I can work again. Months now since my last incident. She sees me toppling at times and seems to pluck me from the precipice. A word, a look, an action. Interjection. A kiss perhaps. She breathes new life. Lips locked, reanimation. Anchors me.

I asked her again, in the park, soon after we began. She

hugged her knees and looked at me from beneath black bangs, long fingers laced in front of her. Donal tumbled to her left inside a sandpit.

'I have no choice,' she said.

'But there are always choices.'

She smiled at me, a half smile, put her chin on her knees and cocked her head. 'You think so?'

And still I call the wrong name. Always choices. After midnight, deep in her room, Caroline's spectre surfaces. Voyeur, uninvited, I stumble upon her behind my eyelids or find her in the face of my lover. Rita holds my head and whispers, murmured consolation, moving gently as I close my eyes and shudder to conclusion. Guilty climax, collapsed sobbing, I will feel her hands soft on me and hear her voice come soothing. 'It's okay. Brandon. It's okay.'

'Don't get me wrong, dear boy,' says Gerald in his living-room, dressed in plain pyjamas. 'I think it's wonderful that you've found love. But doesn't it bother you? Her profession?' He puts a hand on my arm and leans towards me, conspirator, whispering, 'I mean . . . the men. You know?'

'I have my own incubus,' I tell him, handing him a bag of toys.

'As do we all,' he says, sensing this discussion is over. Babysitter, he leads me to the door.

*

It is asparagus season. At six o'clock, Horst and I shuffle amid a tangle of Turkish migrant workers on the footpath, waiting for the minibus. By seven we are transported. South of the city, bent, we advance sideways along the drills of sandy earth, like crabs. The sun beats on our backs. By midday, standing causes fingers of fire to flare along knotted muscles. We stay crouched, afraid to straighten, sweat dripping on our forearms. Home at six-thirty, I lie on the floor and feel my tendons tighten. Rita peels bundles of asparagus in the kitchen. We eat at seven. Afterwards I shower and dress, preparing for work at the Irish pub. When I kiss Donal goodnight he is bathed, squeaky clean, and smells of soap. Horst stands him in the middle of my living-room and dries his hair with a hand-towel. I close the door on his squeals and giggles, slipping quietly away. The pub is hot and smoky. I stand behind the bar handing flat pints of Guinness to the heaving throng. My back aches when I bend to change the barrel. I clean the toilets at two, before I leave. There is a pungent smell, ammoniacal. It is asparagus season.

*

'My mother was German,' I tell Rita, by way of explanation. 'It's not so strange that I should end up here. When my father died, I felt somehow . . . disjointed. Incomplete. As if a circle needed closing. My mother left her home when she was young. A temporary separation. But he held her, made her stay. Forced her to be Irish. She spoke to me in German when I was a child. My mother's tongue in whispers. *Do not tell your father.* I think she never quite got over leaving. I suppose that's what I felt. When he died a bond broke, releasing her too late. I came here for her. Returned on her behalf.'

I am lost then, remembering her. Remembering myself. Her, speaking in her native tongue, and me, a child, tongue-tied, mute until I am four. *Do not tell your father.* Confused, words swam inside me that could not be released. Hard words, guttural, made pliant by the softness of her. Him, all nasal, elongated, different, returning, half-cut some nights, to ask if I am stupid. Later, when the spaces came, I sat in silence, drooling maybe, until his eyes bored into me and roused me from my lethargy or her cold hand caressed me into consciousness. *Is that child stupid or what?* His voice, slurred and booming between pots and pans in the kitchen, still disturbs my sleep at times.

She loved her language, dormant until me. And with it she painted pictures of her homeland, rolling forests and castles, majestic, overlooking rivers. She held me in her arms, kissing my hair, while her husband worked, and together we were transported. Her fugitive words propelled us into an alternative reality, an existence unequivocally ours. When he returned we hid our guilty secret at the dinner table, silent, watching him eat, my mother's metamorphosis complete. She became a dowdy housewife, servile, attentive to his every need. A finger pointed, she would pass the butter or the salt.

Tucking me into bed, she smiled and kissed my forehead. 'I cannot explain to you,' she whispered, her face close to mine, 'what is here.' She held a hand over her heart, staring at me earnestly. Then she moved even closer, her knees cracking on the carpet. She nuzzled into my hair, breathing deeply, savouring the freshness of her child. She closed her eyes and I could tell that she had found her beloved forests in my scent. She stood erect, her strength restored, and touched my face. 'Sleep now, Brandon.'

She left me then, returning to her husband, and I could see her shoulders slumping as she stepped across the threshold.

*

Rita came for us early on Saturday morning. 'Come on,' she said, dangling a car key in front of me, 'we're going for a drive. Gerald said that we could use his car and I borrowed a child-seat from Frau Fischer.'

'Where are we going?' I asked.

'Home,' she said, and leaned over to kiss my cheek. 'It's a long drive. You boys should have a pee before we go.'

We packed quickly, gathering Donal's paraphernalia. 'I didn't know that you could drive,' I said in the garage, with Donal already strapped aboard.

'I can't,' she said, handing me the key. 'But you can.'

It took the best part of a day to drive to Dresden. The *Autobahn* stretched endlessly, grey concrete slipping by, a blur. Tyres whining, the Fiesta's small engine, high-pitched, complained when asked to pass heavy vehicles on hills. Caught, sometimes, we tacked along grooves cut by lorries in the slow lane, the steering wheel pulling at my hands. Donal slept for long periods in his child-seat, sweaty hair matted against his head, a blue shoe stuck into the back of the driver's seat. Or, awake, he chatted with Rita, turned towards him, a hand hanging over the back of her seat, or stretching, tickling. Their laughter was infectious.

I took a wrong turn and we ended up approaching from the east. We crossed the Elbe on a suspension bridge; Loschwitz, the blue wonder, once green paint turned blue with age. Donal craned his neck, trying to see the river flowing beneath us. 'We're nearly there,' I told them, and caught Rita's hand where it rested in her lap. I looked at Donal in the rear-view mirror and he grinned at me, chocolate smudged across his cheek.

On the way into the centre we passed row after row of apartment blocks, built during communist rule. The faceless buildings depressed me with their oppressive greyness. Rita had booked us into a pension in the Neustadt and we were forced to cross the river again, going north. To our left the restored splendour of the Semper Opera and the Catholic cathedral dominated the skyline, lit up orange and green in the gathering twilight. I parked in a cul-de-sac and took our overnight bag from the boot, slinging it across my shoulder. My hands were shaking. Rita lifted Donal and sat him on her hip, looking at me across his head, her eyes searching my face.

'Are you okay, Brandon?'

'Yes. Of course. Just tired.' But I could not quell the sense of apprehension that had been growing in me for the last two hundred kilometres. I was here to take my mother's spirit home.

'Where is this, Papa?' Donal asked, rubbing tiredly at his eye with the back of his hand, his chin nestled against his chest.

'This is where my mother is from, Donal.'

'Is my mammy here too?'

'No. Your mammy isn't here.' I put my hand on his head and tossed his hair. He yawned, weary from the travelling, and put his cheek against Rita's shoulder. 'Come on,' I said. 'Let's go inside.'

Later, I sat on the bed, Donal stretched out, asleep beside me. I watched Rita unpack our bags, facing away from me. She hummed softly to herself, holding shirts in front of her and carefully wiping away wrinkles with her hand before she hung them in the wardrobe. When she bent to take a blouse from her bag, her hair fell loose across her face and I watched her absent-mindedly brush a strand back behind her ear, a half-smile playing on her face.

'I'm glad you made me come here,' I said quietly.

She straightened and turned towards me, her smile widening. 'I had to,' she said, shrugging her shoulders. 'It's important.'

I stood up and put my arms around her. She leaned against me, the blouse hanging by her side, and when she looked up at me, still smiling, I kissed her gently on the lips. 'Thank you,' I said.

She stayed with Donal, leaving me alone to discover the city. I walked beside the river and across Augustusbrücke to the Altstadt. Half-way across the bridge Zwinger came into view, at angles to the opera house, the sandstone walls alive with the sculpture of Permoser. I walked towards the centre of the old town, away from the Theaterplatz. I was struck by the uneasy quietness of the place, the blackened walls, towering, beautiful and sinister, a constant reminder of what had gone before. Ghosts hovered in the baroque buildings, living in the eaves, spinning in the architecture, watching. Unforgotten.

I found the ruins of the Frauenkirche, Our Lady's Church, pounded into submission on the night between the thirteenth and fourteenth of February, 1945. It was surrounded by a low wall awash with molten candle wax. A monument, there was little left, just jagged concrete fingers, twisted and cracked, pointing. And cherubs, angel faces, broken and scarred, dotted through the ruins. Incongruous. It was a tombstone, a reminder. But cranes stood like sentries, black shadows, still against the night sky. Rebuilding had begun. Reunified, Frauenkirche was destined to become a testament to German engineering, not the dead.

I wondered if my grandparents had stood here, caught, perhaps, frozen on their way to the bomb shelters, like rabbits in the headlights of Arthur 'Bomber' Harris's Valentine's Day massacre. Perhaps they held hands, knowing that flight would not save them, and watched their city crumble. Maybe they looked into each other's eyes for a final time as a thundering waterfall of death fell all around them. Bodies brushed them but, buffeted by wild-eyed panic, they clung to each other, ignoring the screams, until their passion for each other calmed them and they gave themselves up to the howling whirlwind of incineration. Did their thoughts turn to her? Did they think of her, their child, surrounded by foreigners, alone? Did they bend their heads in prayer for her, submitting to His will, until a fireball swept over them, devouring the flesh from their bones? Their city of art and culture was swelled to bursting point with wounded German, American and British soldiers, Allied prisoners of war and refugees, fleeing a rampant Red Army. Its cries went unheard within the maelstrom of destruction as it buckled beneath the wrath of Hitler's enemies.

I walked back towards the river, my footsteps echoing in the deserted streets. My grandparents died here. Two. Two among the thousands. Two. Their screams were never heard. How could they be, among the two-and-a-half-thousand tons of high explosive and incendiary devices raining from the night sky? But war is kind to victors. Heroes, whose aim it was to break a nation's spirit. They would make the German population homeless. Create a path for Stalin from the East. But the countless corpses found new homes beneath the rubble. Two. Insignificant. There was a war to be won.

A young girl lay sleeping in an Irish coastal town while her parents lay down for the last time in a city on fire from end to end. I stood beside the Elbe, where American planes are said to have machine-gunned survivors on the following afternoon. I wept for my grandparents. I wept for my mother. I wept for innocence.

IV

We are finding pathways, each of us compensating for another. Gerald speaks too much. Horst not enough. Rita brings a tenderness that soothes us all. And me? I bring the child that binds us all together. He clambers on to a knee, reaches up and twists a nose. *Horse.* The big East German's smile illuminates the room, pockmarked skin blushing and crinkling, all at the same time, acknowledging us, his awkwardness dissipating. He knows that we do not need him to speak. Or playing peekaboo with Gerald, making it all right to be a child. Delighted screams meet overdone theatrics. Gerald finally finds an audience. He has a fan. Sleeping in my lap, then, his arms folded under him, his regular breathing calming me. I realise that I am a father. This realisation gives me purpose, makes me whole. I look across the room at Rita sitting cross-legged on the floor, her chin in her hands, hair falling around her forearms, faraway. She watches him. Always.

Sometimes I lie beside her and see a long brown limb, extended, falling from a sheet. A leg, perhaps. I see a child, fourteen, hungry on the streets of Sao Paolo. White teeth flash in the sunlight, a beacon for lonely tourists. European businessmen, shoes stolen on the beach, come looking for consolation before they phone their wives. I see them glistening in the half-dark, sweat beading between bristles. Fat men grunting. Humping in public lavatories and alleyways, their trousers around their ankles, pale haunches quivering. All for the price of dinner for two. *How do you like it? What do you want me to do?* But her sister dies anyway. One more ten-year-old with needle tracks superimposed on black and blue, battered veins. Who cares?

She watches him. Always.

*

When Horst arrives for dinner Gerald greets him at the door with open arms, a drink in hand and mischief on his mind. Horst shrinks away, wondering, maybe, if flight would be the prudent course of action. But Gerald's voice holds him. 'Horsty, baby,' booming around the corridor. Horst steps inside and closes the door quickly, a blush climbing up his cheeks. Gerald, seemingly oblivious, throws an arm around his shoulders and steers him towards the living-room. Just inside, they stand beside each other, Gerald grinning from ear to ear and Horst, downcast, his cap hanging in front of him, twisting slowly in gnarled fingers. 'Look,' Gerald cries, 'the gang's all here!' Donal, caught up in Gerald's enthusiasm, bounds across the room to meet them. Rita stands and leads Horst to a chair.

'All right, Horst?' I say quietly, ignoring everyone but him. He nods, grateful for my words to focus on. Horst does not like large movements. He is a private man.

'So, Horst,' beams Gerald, crossing his legs in his customary armchair, 'tell us about your day.' His slacks are neatly creased, blue beneath an orange polo shirt. He balances his gin-and-tonic on the arm of his chair. His silver hair shines in the white light thrown by the standing lamp behind him. There is a pink freshness about him, skin gleaming, rosy-cheeked from the alcohol and quinine water. Horst stares at him blankly, his trousers looking like they have been slept in.

'Come now, Horsty. Don't be shy.' Gerald bends forward in his chair, his head cocked, an eyebrow raised.

Horst's mouth opens but no sound comes. His eyes flick from me to Rita and back again. Donal kneels at his feet looking into his face, his feet splayed either side of him. One sock trails along the floor, barely clinging to his heel. 'I . . .'

'Horst,' Rita moves between him and his tormentor, 'would you like a beer?'

'Yes.' Relief washes over him. '*Danke*, Rita.'

'It's Gerald's round,' I say, handing him my glass. 'Another gin for me, and don't forget to change to lemon.'

Gerald rises, reluctantly, taking the glass from my outstretched hand. 'Now I'll never know about the trials and tribulations of Horsty's *jour*,' he sighs and wanders towards the kitchen.

Later, when we are washing up, I turn to Gerald. 'Why do you do that?'

'What, dear boy?' His eyes are wide behind his glasses, his innocence magnified by the lenses.

'You know . . . Horst. Why do you embarrass him like that?'

Gerald smiles devilishly, scrunching up his features. 'Oh, I love to tease him,' he says, barely concealing his delight.

'Well you shouldn't. It makes him uncomfortable.'

'Oh, don't be such a fusspot, Brandon.' Gerald flicks a tea towel at me. 'I have so few pleasures left. Besides, he's so easy to wind up.'

'I just think . . .'

'I know what you think, Brandon,' Gerald interrupts me, 'but you don't have to protect him. Whatever you may think, I like Horst and Horst likes me. He likes being teased.'

'Oh come on!'

'But he does.' Gerald leans towards me and fixes me with

an earnest stare, the bulb above the sink reflected in his glasses. 'It makes him feel part of something, Brandon, not just tolerated. It makes him feel like he belongs. Ultimately, isn't that what we all crave?' He leaves the question hanging between us. I move my hands in the soapy water, feeling knives and forks shift beneath the bubbles. Gerald lifts a plate from the draining-board, shakes it, and starts to wipe the suds from it. 'Look, Brandon,' he says, 'Horst is a quiet man. I know that. But I'm not about to let him shrink inside himself. If he was that uncomfortable he wouldn't come here, would he?'

I have misjudged the man. Gerald is still mothering all of us.

*

Donal's growth continues to astound me. His personality blossoms as the months pass. Phrases gradually come together, sentences escaping from him, surprising sometimes, an infant intellect developing. He switches easily from German to English and back again, bilingual before he's three. He is becoming something more than an extension of me, and more than a mother's after-image. Questions come more frequently, confusing me at times. So much I do not know, and it takes a child to show me.

One night he climbs between us, nightmare tossed. I wake to find him next to her, his dark curls fluttering in her breath, his eyes half closed, white slits, like hers. Her arm has found its way around him in sleep. They are peaceful, like siblings, heartbeats locked together. I lift myself on to an elbow and watch them. Her eyes open to discover him, and she smiles at me across the swell of his cheek. 'Like our child,' she whispers, and I nod. He stirs, his thumb going to his mouth, and nestles against her.

That afternoon is rain-strewn. Donal watches videos

upstairs with Gerald. When I make love to her no images appear. Afterwards I touch her cheek gently, pulling a strand of hair from her mouth, and she smiles at me, sensing something changed. My eyes are here, for her alone.

'Rita,' I say, and her smile widens. 'Rita.' She shifts her weight under me and puts her arms around my waist, squeezing. She starts to move, slowly at first, and I feel myself harden again inside her. And later, when she gasps and bends her hard body under me, her fingernails digging into my shoulders, it is still her face that I see.

*

Gerald takes me playing golf, sneaking me, a novice, on to the course. *His handicap? Have you seen his swing?* From the first tee, my drive bisects the fairway, two hundred meters, dead straight, with a three-wood. Gerald whistles. 'You're sure you haven't played this game before?'

'It's a bit like hurling.'

'Not at all, dear boy. This is not a pagan sport.'

Gerald hits a driver, passing my ball by some twenty meters. His swing has narrowed with age and he lunges forward just before impact but the distance is still there, power in his forearms. He grunts with satisfaction, craning his neck to see the ball descend, take a hard bounce on the frosty ground and leap forward towards the green. 'Topspin, don't you know,' he grins at me. He must have been good when he was younger.

We crunch together through the silver-topped grass, me with my rented clubs slung across my shoulder, Gerald dragging a golf-trolley, his woollen hat pulled down around his ears.

'It's nice out here,' I tell him.

'Yes. Quiet this time of year. No fair-weather golfers. There you are,' he says, indicating my ball. 'I'd say a good firm four-iron.' He breathes deeply and slaps his hands against his thighs while I extract the club. 'This is the life, Brandon, eh?'

I take a long swing at the ball. The club head bounces off the top of it and sends it scampering a few feet in front of me and to my left, into the light rough. 'Your head, Brandon, your head,' he says in mock exasperation, 'I told you. You simply must keep your head still.'

By the fifth hole he is so far ahead that we have given up keeping score. Three from a bunker just short of the fourth green, convincing me that I have much to learn. 'A triple bogey seven,' says Gerald, looking at me over his glasses. 'Or was it eight?'

'We are so lucky,' he says, after holing a ten-foot birdie putt on the par-five sixth.

'Well you are, anyway, I say.'

'No, Brandon. I'm serious,' he says, retrieving the flag and waiting for me to hole out. 'Look around. Smell the air.'

I miss from three feet. 'Shut up for a minute, Gerald, would you?' I get it coming back. 'Nine.'

'Brandon, let me ask you something.' He replaces the flag and catches my arm, solemn now. 'Are you happy?'

'Yeah. I suppose.'

'No, really. Think about it . . . Can you truly say that you are happy?' He squeezes my forearm, his grip hard and bony through my jumper.

'Yes, Gerald. Now that you mention it, I can. And you?'

'That's the point, my boy,' he says, his eyes glistening. "For the first time in my life I can honestly say that I am as happy as . . . ' He pauses, searching for a word.

'A pig in shite?'

'Yes.' He laughs. 'That's it. True Irish eloquence. I am as happy as a pig in shite.'

'I'm glad, Gerald. You're a good man. You deserve happiness.'

'Not everyone is lucky enough to get a second chance, Brandon.' He touches my cheek fondly, his fingers cold in the morning air. 'Thank you for mine.'

'I did nothing, Gerald.'

'Oh no, my boy. You are so wrong. You have done more for me than you can ever know. You and that imp of yours. I just wanted to say it.'

'Thanks, Gerald. It means a lot.'

He pats my shoulder and nods towards our golf clubs. 'Shall we continue?'

'Aye, why not?'

As I hoist my bag on to my shoulder he speaks again, cautiously, feeling his way. 'I haven't heard you mention Caroline in quite some time.'

'No.' I adjust the strap on my shoulder, looking at the ground.

'Forgive me . . . Are you over her?'

'No . . .' I look at him, motionless, his right hand still on the flagpole, his putter hanging from his left. 'But I'm past her.'

'Rita is very special, Brandon. Delicate and tragic, I know, but very special. To have found that kind of love . . .' He shakes his head. 'Some people never find love, Brandon, but you have found it twice. As I said, we are so lucky.'

*

Horst stands beside my son in autumn, surrounded by leaves. Six foot three and gaunt, he puts his hand on the boy's head, a gesture of affection. His thin wrists extend from his jacket, red-raw in the cold sunlight. He reminds me of my grandfather. Silent. Donal takes a moment to look up at the man and smile ferociously. He wears a padded anorak, bought with pooled resources, Horst and Rita. His mittens were knitted by Frau Fischer on the second floor. He returns his full attention to his tricycle. It's hard to find a foothold when you're three.

I watch them from Gerald's kitchen window, a wineglass in my hand. Rita reads quietly at the table. Gerald bustles about in chef's hat and apron, his sneakers squeaking on the polished floor, utensils filling both his hands. He pauses, red-faced, pushing his glasses up on his nose with a little finger, and looks at me. He has left a floury mark on his nose.

'Tell Lurch that lunch is almost ready,' he says, waving a spatula at the window.

This is my family.

V

There comes a lucid moment when I wake and hear them huddled in the dark. Three children breathing, locked together in a far-flung corner of the room. An image is burned in my brain, ostensibly indelible. Her, answering questions.

'So tell us, Mrs Marlowe.' Caroline smiles. Her name, granted, but wildly unfamiliar. She has not been called that in so long. A sergeant holds a stubby pencil in a calloused hand, hovering, expectant, seeking answers. 'Where would your husband have gone?'

She knows. Knows me better than anyone. She will tell them. She knows where I was happy. And they will chase me, now they know where I am going.

We are fugitives.

*

Gerald's death seemed like a betrayal. 'I'm sixty-four,' he told me in September. 'Tired and retired.' We found him cold and lifeless on Christmas morning, lying on the floor, curled around a gin-and-tonic, surrounded by gifts wrapped for us. Rita took Donal to the kitchen while I knelt beside the body, feeling redundantly for the pulse I knew I would not find.

'Oh, Gerald,' I asked his lifeless eyes through tears, my fingers buried in his cold flesh. 'Why now? Why now when everything was starting to make sense?'

The ambulance arrived an hour later. They strapped him to a stretcher and covered his face.

'How old was your father?' asked a medic, taking down details on a clipboard.

'Sixty-four,' I said, feeling the tears well up again. 'My father was sixty-four.'

Gerald would have liked that.

*

We bury him between the years, temporal no man's land. Just us. We are Gerald's family and friends. Gathered by the grave in snow, we breathe plumes of grief across his coffin and leak cold tears. After he is lowered we begin our painful journey home. New Year without him.

We pause with the car door open, Rita, Donal and me. Horst remains beside the grave, weeping. He pulls his trumpet from beneath his coat and raises it to his lips, his long, black coat stark against the frozen landscape, a tragic silhouette. As the quivering uncertain notes of 'The Last Post' drift across the graveyard to us Donal begins to cry.

*

'What will you do with the money?' Rita asked in January.

'Nothing,' I told her. 'It isn't mine. It's Donal's. He left it to Donal. I've put it in a trust fund.'

But my plans were already forming. I had kept a little of the money – just enough. Not selfish, not for me. Yet I knew enough of her to anticipate the pain that I was about to cause her. I could not look her in the eye, and she knew enough of me to sense that I was hiding something. She also knew enough to let me be. I would deal with open issues in my own time.

My own time came in the fleetingness of February. Big changes made in the shortest of months. Quick and painless, like extracting a tooth. Quick, but abscesses are nasty little bastards. She knew before I told her, had guessed what I would do.

'I want him to be Irish,' I said, simply, holding her hand in Gerald's kitchen, surrounded by packing boxes and transformation. She nodded, biting her lower lip, her face angled to the floor, making it impossible for me to read her features. 'Please come with us, Rita. Please.' And even though I knew what she would say, though the knowledge lodged heavily in my chest, I dared to hope that the transience of Gerald's home would instil in her a sense of endings which would enable her to start again.

'I can't,' she said. 'You know that, don't you?'

'No. I don't know any such thing.' I felt a hand closing on my heart, squeezing. A foot of snow outside was not enough to make me numb. 'We belong together.'

'Here,' she said sharply, 'We belong together *here*.' She looked at me, a sadness in her eyes. 'This is where it works. This time, this place.' She stroked the back of my wrist gently with her free hand. 'When you go back to Ireland everything will change. Our relationship would not work there. You know that. I'm black. A black whore. Imagine me in Ireland.' She laughed bitterly. 'Here we are anonymous. It would never work there.'

'We'll make it work. Come with us.' But I knew that she was right. I had known it all along. I felt a knife turning in me. My eyes burned.

'Apart, you belong there and I belong here. That's how it is, Brandon. We can't change that.' She withdrew her hand from mine, a leave-taking, and stood and walked to the window. I sat, my feet flat, my hands hanging limply between my legs.

'You're right, Brandon,' she said, fingering the blinds. 'It's the right thing to do. It's brave of you. Donal needs to know what it is to be Irish.'

'It doesn't feel like the right thing now.' My voice sounded wooden to my ears.

'No. But it will in time. I'll pray for you. At Mass.'

I felt a tear slip from my eye and trickle down my cheek. Sundays would seem empty now, our peaceful time disturbed by vacant yearning. I brushed at my cheek, sniffing quietly. 'I don't want to go.'

'You have to,' she said, her back to me, snowflakes falling like wet feathers beyond her. 'Just go, Brandon. Go.'

I left her at Gerald's kitchen window, her hand curled in the drawstring, her forehead pressed against the cold glass. A passing car threw shadows on the wall and made a halo for her out of frozen snowflakes, like dried flowers sliding on the window-pane.

*

Horst drove us to the airport in Gerald's car, snow-chains clanking like old ghosts on deserted Sunday streets, fifteen below. His pale hands looked like oversized bird claws on the steering wheel, his trumpeter's fingers drumming a distant beat as pale green eyes, elevated at intervals, divined directions from blue signposts as they floated overhead. From time to time he rubbed at his nose with the back of his sleeve. On straight stretches I noticed him watching Donal in the rear-view mirror. The boy sat quietly with his seatbelt on, uncomprehending. Good German, I thought.

He left us at the set-down area. Partings should be easier

with tannoy systems urging you along. A silent man, Horst stood struggling, his mouth opening, awkward, like a fish flopping on a bank. Unfolded from the car he seemed incongruous. Gerald's final joke. *To Horst I leave my car, an old Fiesta.* Behind the wheel the man became a cluster of angles, arms and legs jumbled, his head bent in supplication. Now his dark trousers hung loose around him and his Adam's apple bobbed furiously as he hoisted our baggage from the boot.

'Here, Horst. Let me help you.'

'No.' The word came cracked, forced, accompanied by a hand held up to me. Something that he had to do, his eyes averted.

He piled the cases on the pavement, then lifted Donal in his thin arms and hugged him fiercely, his eyes squeezed shut. He kissed my son's hair and muttered something in his ear. Donal beamed and leaned back, looking into the man's face. 'I love you too, Horse,' he said, and I felt my heart twist sideways. I moved away to find a trolley.

Baggage loaded, we shook hands, the strength of his grip surprising me, as always.

'I'll miss you, Horst,' I said.

'Yes,' he said. 'Goodbye, Brandon.' I tried to pull away but he held on to my hand, his long face troubled, trumpeter's lips pursed, ruby red in the freezing afternoon. 'She loves you, Brandon,' he said at last.

'I know.'

He let go of my hand, tousled Donal's hair and put his hands in his pockets.

'Goodbye, Horst,' I said.

He looked at me for a long moment, pondering again. When he spoke, his voice was thick with emotion. 'I think you are a fool,' he said, and climbed back into his car, bending his frame and folding his limbs. I saw him wipe at his nose again with the back of his hand. As he pulled away from the kerb the streetlights came on and I thought that I saw a liquid film across his eyes. Donal stood waving at the small green car as the brakelights flashed, it mounted a speed bump, accelerated and disappeared in the distance, its oversized occupant hunched behind the wheel, mourning the loss of two more hard-won friends. Fiesta.

MOSES

I

Innocent. Childlike. Slumber. These three, family three, destroy my faith. Touch her shoulder, drag her into daylight's yawn. Look into her eyes. Beautiful eyes. Dark lashes brush brown pupils awake. Brothers beside her, flanking. Two to protect her. Family. Three.

'Shush.' I put my fingers gently to her lips. Black fingernails shame me, stark against her skin. 'You must be quiet.' Whisper. 'Wake the boys. We have to go.'

She nods, hears the rustling outside. Or is it in my head? I thought I saw the shadows. She turns to Peter, shaking him awake. I grunt and shuffle back across the rubble, returning to my vigil.

Pale sunlight edges its way through broken window frames, dawn clawing its way into the room. They rise now, like Lazarus, and join me, peering into the woods. She puts her hand in mine, her slender fingers firm against my palm. I look down at her, blond hair, halo, surrounding silent questions on her face. Her eyes. The darkness of her eyes.

'They'll be here soon,' I tell her. 'Better move.'

'I'm hungry, Johnny.' William's chin trembles, as if he is about to cry.

'I'll get you something later. Speed. It's all about speed. I saw the shadows. We have to stay ahead.'

I lift her then, wrapping her in my coat. It is cold this morning. Her arms go round my neck, her head falls on my shoulder. Weary. Tired of running. At times I am repulsed by

them, by what they have done. Powerless then, I am drawn to
them again. Her eyes find mine. Her eyes. And I am overwhelmed
by love for her again. Like them. What would you do for her,
Johnny? How far would you go? Like them.

*

Crunchy kicks me into consciousness, his toes nudging at
my feet.

'Moses. Wake up, you fuckin' fucker.'

I am awake, eyes opening, dragged into another day. I
had dreamt of numbers. Equations swimming like ethereal
amoebae in my brain. I remember numbers. Logic. The
numbers making sense. *One and one.* What I was before.
Before this. Christ, if only I could remember. *One and one.*
If only it would all make sense. Sometimes I dream in
German. I know that it is German when I wake and foreign
words come tumbling from my mouth. Understood. Lyrical.
Like *Frühling* and *Herbst.* Cabalistic words that mundify
the seasons. Start again. Numbers. *Eins. Zwei.* Still making
sense.

'Moses. Are you awake, for fuck's sake?' Crunchy prods
me with a crutch now, impatient.

'Were going to have to do something about your vocabu-
lary, Crunchy,' I say, sitting up, emerging from a tangle of
cardboard boxes, plastic bags and dreams. This is my reality.
Discarded, I lie wasted in an alleyway.

'What the fuck are you talkin' about?' Crunchy bends
over me, his skinny forearms extending from his crutches
like turkey bones picked clean at Christmas. His breath is
foul in my face.

'Never mind.' I sigh and climb to my feet, stretching the
stiffness out of my bones.

'You're fuckin' mad. Come on, we have to go.'

He hobbles ahead of me, towards St Stephen's Green, his crutches pinging on the pavement. The extension to the N11 made Crunchy redundant. He used to sit in a ditch on the old Wicklow road, waiting for the right car. When the opportunity presented itself, he would fling himself in front of slow moving traffic, exploding from the foliage like a startled pheasant to plunge beneath the wheels. Insurance companies pay out big for broken limbs. *'The fuckin' county council,' he spat once as we shared a doorway and a bottle. 'The bastards built a motorway right along my spot. The cars go too fuckin' fast now. Sure they'd kill you if they hit you. And the drivers can see you from a mile off. Inconsiderate bastards . . . '*

He stops suddenly and turns towards me, hunched over. His ragged suit hangs from him like a sack on a scarecrow. His torn left shoe smiles up at me where the sole has come away from the upper. I stand still over my makeshift bed.

'Do you want your fuckin' breakfast or not?' he asks, before turning and scurrying down the alleyway, muttering to himself.

Muttering to himself. Like me. I begin my daily routine. 'Moses,' I say quietly. 'One and one. Who's Moses? Who *is* Moses? Moses. That's me. Moses. One and one.'

*

I have become direct. The fear has left me. I look at faces where before I looked at shoes. And faces slide away sideways to stare in shop windows, watching reflections of me passing. They do not want to see the real me, so they settle for images in glass, brittle, easily broken. They ignore the flesh and bone, the oak I have become.

At first I revelled in their discomfort, the seeming reluctance to touch me. I grew my beard and learned to snarl when approached. Mad dog. Paths appeared before me as I walked. Openings. Throughways through crowds. More Moses.

When I drink it takes the edge off my sense of loss. Off my sense. I stand, stained and grubby in Grafton Street, drinking from a bottle in a brown paper bag. Free to rant. *One and one.* If you stand like this, in the middle of the street, your feet rooted, your arse cocked at a jaunty angle and your fists rigid at your side, they all take notice, watching cautiously from the corners of their eyes. Bellow. *'Fuck off.'* It is amazing how they scatter. Like flocks of birds migrating, they wheel together, dissipating. Toy policemen, boys, come with solemn faces and calm, quiet voices. Reluctant hands brush against your elbows. 'Come on now, move along. No one wants a scene.'

But everybody does. I am watched with morbid fascination. *What makes a man sink so low? There but for the grace of God . . .* Counting. *One and one.* A girl pushes fifty pence into my hand. 'Buy yourself a cup of tea, love.' She is twenty-one or -two, perhaps. Before I think to thank her she is gone, dissolving back into the crowd of shoppers and Spanish students. She is expediently absorbed. Back where she belongs. A prodigal, returned. The policemen stand a few paces from me, at angles, carefully inattentive, their visors pulled low over watchful eyes. One of them clears his throat and chances a glance in my direction. I smile at him and he quickly turns away, blushing faintly.

'Me arse,' I shout, swinging my paper bag, and move slowly through the parting sea of faces, each pair of eyes detaching itself dutifully from my progress, falling away in sequence, like synchronized swimmers entering a pool. *One and one.*

I have become a thing apart, an oddity, a freak. When I

sleep, I sleep in shadows, out of doors in doorways.

*

'What were you, Crunchy? Before this. What were you?'

Crunchy regarded me and raised a cigarette stub to his mouth, his fingers clenched around it like a backward claw. He breathed the smoke deep into his lungs, leaving only vapour trails to curl from his nostrils and the corners of his mouth. He was sitting in a corner, leaning against the wall, his feet drawn up in front of him, exposing thin hard shins with their network of white scars. His shoes were placed carefully beside him, a sign of trust for me, perhaps, and his toes stuck out through holes in his socks. He snorted and spat heavily into a pile of crumpled newspaper.

'I was a fuckin' choirboy,' he said, and started to laugh. 'Where the fuck did I get you?'

The candle flickered between us, draughts causing mayhem with the flame. We had broken in that afternoon, pulling the boards from a back window and searching for a room with a halfway decent roof. The building was condemned. Like us.

'Seriously, Crunchy. How do people get like you and me?'

'I think myself it's all to do with natural talent,' he said. 'But then I could be fuckin' wrong.'

'Come on, Crunchy. I want to know. Did you have a family? A girl? A mother? I want to know.'

'No. You don't.' He was serious suddenly, his eyes flashing in the half-light. 'Because if you allow yourself to think about it, you'll go fuckin' mad. Survival, Moses. That's what it's all about. Survival. We don't shoot up, we're clean. We're dry tonight and it's pissin' down outside. We're doin' it. We're survivin'. So just don't fuckin' think about it, right?' He leaned his forehead against the heel of his hand, sighing heavily. 'And don't fuckin' ask me to think about it either.' Almost as an afterthought. I couldn't tell whether he was speaking to me or to himself.

We were silent then, listening to the rain drumming on the tin roof, sirens wailing on Sheriff Street. Crunchy looked small and broken in the candlelight, like an injured bird. I almost started to pity him but I knew that if I did I would not see him again. He would be gone before sunrise.

'Do you remember Tony Cascarino?' he asked suddenly. 'The big tall fucker who scored all the goals for Ireland?'

'Aye, I do.'

'That was me.' He hooted with laughter again and threw a shoe at me across the room.

*

He finds me soon after I become this. Lost. I am huddled on a bench in the rain, dripping, as he shuffles by, his crutches sliding on the wet pavement. I see him hesitating, wondering. He stops and turns back, decided.

'Hey. You. What the fuck are you doin' there? Are you fuckin' mad? You'll catch your death.'

Perhaps that's the idea. Perhaps it's all too much. I shiver, staring at him, my teeth chattering, loud in my ears, rain running in icy rivulets from my hair. He is standing on one foot, a newspaper held folded over his head, his elbow at angles to his crutch, like Long John Silver.

'Jaysus.' He hops forward, closer to me, peering through the darkness and rain. 'A new boy. Do you fuckin' come here often?' He laughs loudly at his own joke, looking around as if to see if anyone else has heard him and is bent double by his wit. I continue to stare at him. He waits, wondering, maybe, if I am a deaf mute. 'Ah, fuck ya,' he says, eventually, and swivels on his crutch. He starts to move away, then pauses again and looks over his shoulder at me, the newspaper hanging from his hand, his thumb hooked around the handle of a crutch. 'Come on,' he says. 'I know a place.' I get up and follow him.

He scampers through back streets, previously unknown to me. We do not speak, moving in silence apart from the metallic thwack of his crutches and the grunt forced from him each time he swings himself forward. I have to hurry to keep up.

He introduces me at the hostel. 'This is my friend . . .'

'Moses,' I say. 'His friend Moses.'

'Yeah. Moses. This is my fuckin' friend Moses. Have you any beds?' he says, fishing in his pockets. 'You have to make a donation, like Mass,' he whispers to me. 'Have you a quid?' I look at him blankly and he throws his eyes to heaven. 'Never mind. It's on me. Jaysus.' He pushes two pound coins through the hatch. 'We could do with a couple of fuckin' towels, too, if you have them. It's fuckin' pissin' out there.' He leans on his crutches, waiting, and grins at me.

'My name's Crunchy,' he tells me. 'It's a fuckin' pleasure to meet you.'

*

The first morning, at breakfast in the hostel, he reaches across the table between bites and grips my forearm. 'Stick with me, kid. You'll be fuckin' grand.' The words come strewn among bits of bread. But those brittle, early weeks are torturous. Depression mummifies me, closing on my mind like a black hood. New Year, new life. Auld acquaintance forgot. Tongue-tied and sluggish, I amble through a twilight world. Like limbo. I am suffering for sins I can't remember.

Perhaps it is a part of my penance, not knowing. *Oh my God, I am heartily sorry . . .* But Crunchy goads me to cognisance with his foul-mouth, half-baked truths. Coaxing. Probing. Gentle in his own rough way. He has been here. He knows where the mines lie. *'Lord fuckin' muck,'* he calls me when I turn my nose up at a free dinner. *'Look at you, you scrawny fucker. Like you can afford to be choosy . . .'*

Reluctantly, I venture into pale-lit winter landscapes. First steps. I am an infant, discovering. Grey smoke hangs low, mingling with clouds, motionless against a January skyline. Its stasis petrifies me, hard to get a grip on. I sink into paralysis, resigned. But hidden in the monochrome is substance. Camouflaged concrete. Thawing, I begin to notice and he pushes me, nudging, a coarse yet subtle presence. 'Come on, boy,' he says between the words, 'I will make you live.'

On the Ha'penny Bridge, Crunchy breathes deeply and swings his arms against himself for warmth, his crutches snug under his armpits. 'Smell that?' he asks, fixing me with a watery eyeball. His open palms thump against his shoulders. 'The hops. Guinness's. Lord Jaysus, I'd murder a pint.' Or, slumped against a wall, he stretches his bad leg in front of him, the foot at grotesque angles. Passers-by avert their eyes or offer change, indulgences. He leans towards me, foetid breath, a wicked glint. 'Look,' he nods across my shoulder. I follow his gaze and see tight jeans retreating. He whispers in my ear. 'There's an arse for a lazy mickey, what?'

We have started to travel together, to depend on one another. No. That isn't true. I depend on him. But he might say that we move in the same social circles. He is guarded, though. Afraid. Parts of him off-limits. I watch him sometimes, wondering, the muscles in his jaw bunching as he chews. His eyes distant, his face blank, his hand moving independently, life of its own, rubbing at his nose. And then he catches me. 'What the fuck are you looking at? Did you never see snot before?'

I begin to speak again in more than monosyllables. Questioning. *Who am I? Who is Moses?* I need to know the reasons for my exile. The mumbling begins. Figures. Looking for logic, axioms to cling to. One and one. Signs of madness, yes, and not the first. 'Jaysus, Moses,' he says, 'I liked you better when you hadn't a tongue in your head.'

*

He is there when I awaken, watching me, a frown across his features.

'You were talking in your sleep,' he says. 'You woke me up.'

I feel far from rested. There is a sour taste in my mouth. Like copper, maybe. It must have been the cheap wine.

'Sorry, Crunchy.'

'Don't be.' He is propped on an elbow, his coat around his shoulders, his lower half covered in newspaper. A cigarette butt dangles from his mouth. My head begins to clear, sleep surrendering.

'What was I saying?'

He sucks on the butt, the end flaring red in the slanted morning light that slithers between the window boards. 'I don't know. Something foreign. Fuckin' German or something. Afraid I can't help you out, Sunshine.'

'Shit. I thought . . .'

'You think too fuckin' much, Moses. That's part of the problem. You shouldn't think.' He struggles to his feet, retrieving his crutches from beneath the newspapers. 'Come on, I need a piss.'

He has a variety of hiding places. Homes. Condemned buildings, waste ground, doorways. A man for all seasons, Crunchy calls himself. He doesn't like to sleep out of doors - *I'm a touch delicate, don't you know* - but he only goes to the hostel when he has to. He relishes his freedom. He is content to share this world with me. His half-life. Taking me under his wing. I see him as a bird, sometimes. A crow. Black. Flapping. Coughing. His back bent. *Jaysus.* Laughter mixing with his spasms. Then fluttering away.

'How old are you, Crunchy?' I ask him as we stand side by side, urinating in the alleyway.

'Mind your own fuckin' business,' he says, his fag-butt bobbing between his lips. He breaks wind noisily, shakes himself, and buttons up his trousers.

He must be sixty if he is a day. Deep creases run the length of his face and, when he takes his hat off, his hair, what little remains of it, is steel grey. He has a bulbous nose, broken arteries criss-crossing it, like crimson railway tracks intersecting, or branches. But he knows all the tricks and he is generous with them. He knows the pubs to stand outside at closing time, his cap hanging in his hand, nonchalant, as if he's waiting for his girlfriend. '*God bless you, sir.*' Muttered acknowledgement as burly men fish loose change from the pockets of their jeans, then move off, pulling their padded jackets around their shoulders, clearing their throats, their breath freezing in the midnight air. Crunchy pockets his earnings like a conjuror palming cards, one fluid movement, his cap returned to his head. Perched. 'Come on.' He's off again.

'There's no use beggin' from young fellas,' he tells me, his acolyte. 'They're as likely to give you a kick, the pups.' He knows when to move on, sees gangs shuffling up Grafton Street and vanishes up side streets, his crutches clicking.

Once bitten . . .

'You just have to accept it,' he tells me late at night. 'That's the fuckin' trouble with you, Moses. You keep thinking that this is all just a bad fucking dream or something. It's not. You won't wake up. You have to accept it. Otherwise . . .' He does not finish the thought.

But my recovery begins with an awakening. This time I am dreaming of smooth skin, the nape of a neck, ridges, vertebrae. Cold hands on me and soft, wet kisses. When I open my eyes, the image remains, merging with my consciousness. I am lying on my back with a yellow door stretching above me. *I have been here before. In a former life.*

I am at a nightclub. Leeson Street. The music pounds, vibrating through my senses. My long hair, wet with sweat, keeps getting in my eyes as I shake my head violently to the beat. I feel the bass guitar climb through me, erupting in my chest. It feels good. Young. Just let go. Too many nights spent shuffling self-consciously at parties in some student's flat. Feet like clay betray you, expose your syncopation for a singular deficiency of timing. But here I just let go. Nobody knows me. It doesn't matter what they think or say. The alcohol burns warm inside my stomach, causing slipstreams as I swing my head in slow motion, peppering the floor with perspiration. Suddenly I'm tangled in her handbag. Wound around my feet it trips me, scudding after me across the floor as I try to regain my balance, until I'm sitting on the dance floor, drenched, and howling in hysterical laughter. She folds her long frame over me, smoothing long dark hair behind an ear. And then I see her eyes and I am smitten. Deep dark things, like thick honey, reflecting flashing greens and reds and blues. 'Do you think I could have this back,' she says, unwinding her handbag from my twisted limbs. 'Cheers.' Then she is gone, leaving me uncertain and suddenly sober.

I find her in Abrakebabra, sitting with her friends.

'Hi. Remember me?'

'Oh yeah,' she smiles, 'the handbag snatcher.'

'Sorry about that. No harm done, eh? Can I sit down?'

'It's a free country.' She shuffles along, pushing a sullen redhead before her. I sit beside her, conscious of the sweat drying on my skin.

'I wouldn't have taken you for the sort,' I say.

'What?' Her forehead wrinkles and she snorts a nervous laugh at me. 'What sort?'

'The dance-around-the-handbag sort.'

'Well you never can tell.' Her friends are talking among themselves now, ignoring us. 'You seem a little more in control of yourself.'

'There's nothing like making a complete ass of yourself for sobering you up. I wanted to apologise.'

'For what?'

'You know . . .'

When her friends drift off, to my surprise she stays, sipping coffee with me. Intoxicated by each other now, we reach across the table with our words, a kind of verbal foreplay. She will not say her name. She makes me guess.

'Desdemona.' Deadpan.

She puts the back of her wrist to her mouth and giggles uncontrollably.

'I'm an astronaut,' I tell her, 'a part of Ireland's space programme.'

'I didn't know that Ireland had a space programme,' she says, all mock-wide eyes.

'Yeah, we're going to be the first to send a man to the sun. But don't worry, it won't be too hot, they're sending me at night.'

Giddy, we become easy in each other's company.

'My father was a big pig farmer in Kildare,' she tells me, after some cajoling.

'Wait a minute, wait a minute,' I point a plastic fork at her across the table. 'A big pig farmer . . . Does that mean that he has a big farm with small pigs on it or that he has a small farm with big pigs on it?' She snorts with laughter and slaps at my hand. 'Or could it be that he's a big man with small pigs on a small farm?'

She catches my hand as if she is trying to strangle it. 'Enough already,' she says between gasps for breath. 'Jesus, you're a total moron.'

'Don't call me Jesus,' I say, narrowing my eyes. 'Nobody's supposed to know.'

Later, when I walk her home, we stand on her doorstep kissing. She does not ask me in, not tonight. Before the door clicks closed I put my hand to it, causing her to pause.

'Your name,' I say, 'you never told me your name.'

She smiles, her palm flat against the door jamb. 'Caroline,' she says. 'Caroline Dalton. Goodnight, sweet prince, and all that shite.'

She leaves me standing on her doorstep.

I have been here before. In a former life.

*

He teaches me to survive, this ragged man. Without him I could drown here, surrounded by frightened curiosity. Do I scare them that much? But Crunchy knows the way it is. Dublin belongs to Crunchy. This part of it, a part apart. Discarded. Forgotten. I watch him rooting in a dustbin and I wonder how that fragile frame can contain a heart as large as his. He extracts a pair of ladies' stockings and proffers them, leering, laughing, draping them across his face and hopping up and down. Then, suddenly distracted, he hoists himself on to his crutches and takes off. 'Moses, come on.' A new-found urgency. I follow him at speed along an alleyway and across the green. We were Butch and Sundance once, or could have been. Always in a hurry, Crunchy. Always something waiting around the next corner. But old corners bother me. That is what separates us. 'You can't go back.' Crunchy gets angry at me sometimes. 'There's no fuckin' goin' back. Besides, if the past was that good, what the fuck are you doin' here?' That's why Crunchy must always move on, is always on the move, me slipstreaming. Crunchy is running. I am . . . forgetful.

Shadows come lunging sometimes when I am walking. I flinch. Perhaps a sound escaping from me. An oath. Involuntary. Startled. People see my face and move a little further from my path, uneasy, reluctant to discount a madman's demons. I am never sure what is there and not there. A familiar face in the crowd, disappearing before I reach the spot, or a memory, elusive, like an itch beyond my outstretched fingers. Cold comfort when I curl against the weather in Baggot Street. Her face. Caroline. A light shining from the window of her flat. Shadows. I remember coffee in her living-room and precious little else. Snatches. Phrases of past life. Lives. A family lives there now. I saw them, mother, father, daughter, carry shopping bags upstairs before the door swung shut. And then the light came on. When Crunchy sees me pondering he prods me with a crutch. He seems determined to save me from myself. No going back.

'I need to know, Crunchy.' He looks at me, his chin flecked with spittle, dirty fingernails extended towards me, leaning on a crutch.

'Bollox. If you needed to fuckin' know, you'd know. Maybe you need not to know. Did you ever think of that?'

But the frustration grows in me, the gnawing will not go away.

Sometimes I lose days now but no one notices. What is a day compared to the lives that we have lost? Crunchy may comment. 'Where the fuck have you been?' But then he may have said that anyway. We are displaced, we come and go. We give each other space. Sometimes I feel hands on me, urging me to consciousness, securing me. But when I come round there is no one there, just the faint afterthought of a dark-skinned girl with kind eyes and the sound of water dripping somewhere. Later I will find Crunchy on a park bench, picking at a sandwich, his crutches balanced beside him.

'Where the fuck have you been?'

*

'I had a house,' I tell him. 'A car, a television.' There are things that I remember now. Small things. He leans against the wall, smoking, his eyes guarded.

*

Crunchy has his own nightmares. Sometimes I hear him moaning in his sleep. I turn and see his legs twitching underneath the newspaper, his face contorted. Tears fill the crevices of his face, his hand, unconscious, wiping them away. I can hear the leather of his palm rub rough against his salt-and-pepper stubble. Words come squeezed, grunted denials. Treacherous slumber, he will toss and turn his way towards consciousness. Demons can be hidden in the daylight. He will fart and smile and hobble through the morning, unperturbed. Gap-toothed. Only occasional shadows cross his waking face, like spasms, brief, and casually concealed.

'All right, Moses?' Crunchy is the strong one. Steady on his crutches, he bolsters everybody else, his personal tragedy taboo. I count on that, I know. I use his strength to get me through the day. As if it is real. As if the illusion is convincing. I do not feel guilty about it. Crunchy needs it too, needs to think that I am fooled. We all create our own realities, invent ourselves in the image of what we want to be. Crunchy is larger than life. All bluff and bluster. He skips his way through challenges. Slippery, will-o'-the-wisp, the real Crunchy obscures himself behind the vastness of his public persona . . .

. . . Except at night, when barriers come down. Asleep, his anguish writes itself, unknown to him, in every twisted corner of his body. It speaks in frightened whispers in the dark. A hand closing, knuckles white. Mouth open, lips pulled thin. Loose words released, the pain exposed, *'Oh Jesus . . .'*

In the morning, when he smiles, I will allow him to deceive me. Crunchy lives and breathes within the confines of his wafer-thin disguise. I will not comment on his midnight indiscretions; I am neither comforter nor judge.

'You have to be fuckin' tough,' he tells me, losing patience. 'For Christ's sake, Moses. You have no choice. It's all about survival. This is no life for nancy boys, talkin' about their fuckin' feelings. Memory me arse. It's better that you don't remember. You're the lucky one.'

Crunchy knows how to survive. It is what separates us. He is protected, has acquired a shell. Lessons, hard-learned long ago. Old dreams are buried deep. Some thoughts exist now only deep in his subconscious. Past lives have been smothered, old loves forgotten. New life. What's gone is gone. His real strength comes from resignation, a hopelessness of sorts. *This is what I am now. No going back, move on.* Phoenix.

He can live with that, awake. His consciousness can deal with it. It is what separates us.

*

I can feel my body hardening, the softness of my former life redundant. I am metamorphosing, imago. As if, adult, my history is meaningless. They would accept me here, no questions. And yet I am uneasy. An outcast amongst outcasts. I skirt around the edges of their permanence. Afraid to be assimilated and careful not to ruin their ecosystem. Frailty here, for all their bluster. But Crunchy gives me scope. A bridge, he offers hope and opportunity. I could belong here, a feature of their wasteland. *Crunchy says that it's okay.*

But their sense of self repels me. I am different. Unclean. *I don't know who I am.* Derelict, I lumber here. Ignored at times. Or not. Sometimes they make the effort. 'Give us a kiss,' says Mary, her one good tooth at sea amid her ruddiness. She is overweight and bound in layers of clothing. 'I loves young fellas.'

Crunchy moves easily, achieves a new fluidity. Home away from homeless, trading stories of scabies and body lice. My reluctance is not remarked upon. We are all damaged here. There is no need to exhibit hidden wounds. *'It's understood,' they seem to say. 'You have all the time you need to heal, like all of us before. And when you're ready we will still be here.'*

So Crunchy takes my place and puckers up. 'I loves aul' fellas too,' says Mary, beaming and cupping his buttock, playing to the gallery. Crunchy's follow-up is drowned by hoots and wolf-whistles but a wicked grin is plastered on his face.

*

I remember her in vignettes, each new piece a maddening reminder of a past I need to know.

Shock when she comes home – *home?* – her hair cut tight, dark tresses littering some barber's floor. I loved her hair, the feel of it wrapped around my fingers, her head, heavy in sleep, against my shoulder. There is a new innocence to her. Exposed. Wide-eyed. A roundness in her cheeks that went previously unnoticed. I want to hold her.

Undressing her, the weight of her, the warmth. The pain behind her eyes, the lids descending. How her brow furrows and her mouth opens, rocking. The whiteness of her teeth. And when she falls on top of me, gasping, her shoulder tucked beneath my chin, her breasts are soft against my chest.

She wraps a sheet around herself and sits silhouetted by the window, dark thoughts coursing through her, palpable. I see my hand stretched, touching her shoulder. Ink blots are shadows on the fingers. She turns, half smiles, her knees pulled underneath her chin, head on one side. Her lips touch the back of my hand. Words are left unspoken between us.

I catch her crying and she claims it is the onions. She sniffs and keeps on cutting. The onions count for nothing. I had seen her shoulders shaking when she did not know that I was watching.

Vignettes. Like spider's web, caught, sticky, on evening walks. Tangled, I try to catch the thread that will release me but I am left with only traces. Resonant, perhaps, but only traces, fragments of a past that lingers, shattered, somewhere deep inside my skull. I am like a child, frustrated by a jigsaw, searching for the piece that will complete the puzzle. Shreds of her swim throughout my consciousness. Especially her eyes. Dark eyes, vividly remembered, dripping golden fire. Orbs that I could orbit for a lifetime, unperturbed.

And still each thought of her is incomplete. Caroline

Dalton. Her name is nothing without mine . . . *My wife. She may have been my wife. Mrs Moses* . . . I search the phonebooks in the GPO in vain. She is lost to me.

*

Crunchy told Sheila about me. She found me in Bewleys, drinking coffee.

'Moses?' Her hair was tied back, pretty face. She was in her late thirties; or older maybe, but well preserved. She wore a pair of faded jeans, a green sweat shirt and an old anorak. I looked at her suspiciously, non-committal.

'You are Moses, aren't you?' She sat across from me, uninvited, folding her hands between us on the table. 'My name is Sheila. Your friend Crunchy told me about you.'

'Judas,' I whispered, looking away from her.

'Come on now. Don't be like that.' I could hear the smile in her voice. 'He's worried about you. He's your friend. He just asked me to talk to you, that's all.'

'What are you?' I turned back to her, staring into her face. 'A social worker?' An accusation of sorts.

'I suppose.' She shrugged, shifted her hands on the table, the palms turning upwards, fingertips touching.

'Crunchy should mind his own business,' I said, starting to stand up.

'Please.' She didn't move. If she had touched my arm I might have shook her off and walked away, but the fact that she did not try to stop me made me pause. 'I just want to talk. Can I buy you another coffee?'

'No. Thanks,' I said. But I sat down again. We sat watching each other quietly for a moment. She was giving me time to accept her.

'Like I said, Crunchy is worried about you,' she said at

last, breaking the silence.

'Why?' I sounded gruff, even to myself.

'He says you don't belong here. He says you never will.'

I laughed. 'None of us belong here. None of us deserve to live like this.'

'Some people want to live the way you do, Moses.' She smiled. 'Don't you know that? For some people it's a choice. Free will, you know. It's not for us to judge.'

'Then don't,' I snapped.

'I'm not.' Her face seemed open, her voice was not combative, just like old friends having a philosophical debate over a cup of coffee in Bewleys. 'What can I do to help you, Moses?' she said softly.

'Just leave me alone.'

'I can only help you if you let me, Moses. Why don't you let me. Help me to help you.'

'Christ.' I laughed and glanced across the table at her. 'Psychobabble.'

'Sorry.' She had the good grace to smile sheepishly at me. 'Crunchy says you don't know who you are.'

'None of us do.'

'That's not true, Moses. Crunchy knows who he is. His name is Joseph Fowler. He has to know that to be able to get the dole. What's your name, Moses? Your real name.' I stared at her sullenly, realising that she thought that I was faking, thought that I had chosen to forget, to become detached. 'Let me help you, Moses.' She looked at me earnestly, pleading. 'Let's get you signed on, anyway. It's a start, isn't it? You could use the money. Just tell me your name. That's all you have to do. I'll take care of everything else.'

I sighed and ran a hand across my face. 'What did you say your name was again?'

'Sheila.'

I leaned across the table towards her and looked straight into her eyes. 'Well listen carefully, Sheila,' I said calmly. 'You seem like a nice person. I think your heart is in the right place. Okay? So I'd love to answer your questions. I'd love to know the answers myself. But I don't. I am adrift here. Do you understand that? I'm a castaway. Crunchy says I don't belong, and he's right. I don't belong anywhere. The only way you can help me is if you leave me alone and stop torturing me with the same questions I torture myself with, day in, day out.'

She blinked and looked away from me, leaning on her elbow, her hand covering her mouth. *I noticed a wedding ring on her finger and I thought of Caroline, her face softening when I touched her shoulder, turning from the dishes, leaning in to me . . .* 'I'm sorry,' she said. 'I didn't mean to upset you.'

'I know,' I sighed again. 'It's okay, I'm not upset.'

She fingered a corner of my napkin that peeked over the edge of my saucer at her. I saw her brow furrow, the confusion in her eyes. 'You're not really what I expected,' she said, looking at me.

'We all have our prejudices.'

'Yeah, I suppose . . . Look, if there's anything I can . . .'

'Thanks.' I smiled at her and touched her hand. 'There's nothing anyone can do for me right now.' I drained my coffee cup, stood up, and hoisted my bag on to my shoulder, ready to leave. She remained seated, looking up at me. 'See you around, Sheila.'

'Here,' she held out a card to me. 'I mean it. If there's anything I can do . . .'

I took the card and nodded to her, putting it in my pocket, then began to move away. I hesitated. 'There is one thing,' I said, looking back across an empty table at her.

'What's that?' She put her head to one side, curious.

'Tell Crunchy not to worry.' I winked at her and left her sitting alone with my empty coffee cup.

*

It is cold and Caroline stands close to me, her hands withdrawn, vanished up the sleeves of her coat like shy tortoises. She has wrapped her scarf around her mouth. Desperado. Her eyes are watering and her knees are angled towards each other, knocking almost.

'You're not cold, are you?' I bump her with my shoulder, smiling, my breath freezing and billowing in front of me. She thumps me through her padded sleeve and giggles.

'Whatever gave you that idea? Of course I'm bloody cold. It's freezing.'

'Relax.' I put my hands on her shoulders, looking into her face. 'It's a well-known fact, if you try to bunch up against the cold it just makes it worse. You have to relax. Go with it.'

The wooden works are slippery, silver in the moonlight, and she leans against me as we walk. Full moon, hanging low above the harbour. Bright. Crisp. We leave dark stains, trails along the quays, our footsteps like black holes, following us. Leading to . . .

Her nose is cold against my cheek when I kiss her. Snuffle. Her lips are thin lines, pulled tight, chapped and shivering. Warm chin, recently released from deep protection, and warm moist mouth, inviting.

'This is how I remember it,' I tell her, wrapping my arms around her from behind, her head resting against my shoulder. The bridge stretches to our left. A car crawls, cautious behind us, ice alert. No other sound but our breathing and a television set, too loud somewhere. 'My town. Solitary. Calm water reflecting the lights along the quays. The mudbanks. My footsteps, singular

on cold nights, muffled by the wooden works, softened . . . I could never hate the place, not like the others.'

'Why should you hate it?' She angles her head to look at my face. Her cheeks look bruised in the half-dark. Everything black and white.

'Small town syndrome. It wasn't fashionable to like where you grew up.'

'I don't know,' she says. 'I like your sense of belonging. When Daddy died and Mammy remarried, I lost that. Moving to Dublin . . . You know . . . I feel like I missed out on something, like I lost a part of me. Not just my daddy, something more . . . I . . . I like your sense of belonging.' She twists and puts her arms around me, squeezing. I bend to kiss her, warmer now. Belonging.

My sense of belonging. We began speciously. I am sitting on my bench in Stephen's Green again. Returning. Crunchy is still talking. Crunchy is always talking. The chip bag lies between us, hot. How could she know? I didn't know myself. Home? Belonging? Solitary. Singular. Alone . . . It was not a sense of belonging, it was the safety of solitude she sensed. The comfort of not having to belong. *You have to go with it.*

'I'm from Wexford, Crunchy.'

'What?' He stops talking and looks at me as if I'm mad, as if my proclamation is the ranting of a madman. I can't blame him. Maybe it is.

'I said I'm from Wexford. I don't know how I know it, I just do. I just remembered. Does that make sense?'

Crunchy takes the chip bag from the bench and holds it out to me, offering. 'Eleven,' he says.

'What?' My turn to look at him as if he's mad.

'Eleven. I fuckin' said *Eleven*.' As if I am an annoying child, and deaf at that.

'I know what you said, Crunchy. I just don't know what you mean.'

'It's like this, see?' Crunchy fishes another chip from the bag and pops it into his mouth. 'You're always fuckin' goin' around saying one and one, right?' He chews with his mouth open, the masticated chip white against his black teeth. 'Well one and one is eleven.'

'No. It's two.'

'Not all the time.' He twists back and forth on the bench, shaking his head. 'Sometimes it's fuckin' eleven.'

'You're not making sense, Crunchy.'

'That's the point.' He turns towards me, his eyes bright. 'The answers don't always make sense. Don't you see? For fuck's sake. You'll never see it if you're too busy worrying about fuckin' rules.' He pauses, waiting, then hurries on, impatient. 'Don't think. Just answer. There's two numbers in eleven. What are they?'

'One and one.'

'You see?' He points at me with a limp chip. 'So you're from fuckin' Wexford. Tough break, but why the fuck are you worried about how you know? The important thing is that you do know. Stop trying to make sense of everything. You don't have to. Your fuckin' brain knows that, even if you don't.' *You have to go with it.*

'Crunchy,' I say, reaching for another chip, 'you're not nearly as stupid as you look.'

'Thanks,' he says, and bites into his burger.

*

'Are you sober, Moses?' Sheila bends over me in Grafton Street, shaking my shoulder.

'Yeah. Unfortunately.'

'Where's your other half?' She squats beside me.

'Crunchy? God alone knows.'

'Aye. Well, can I buy you a cup of coffee?'

'What is it with you, Sheila?' I squint up into her face, the cold afternoon light framing her. 'You're always trying to buy me coffee. I thought you were married.'

'I am, Moses,' she smiles. 'Happily. So don't worry, you're safe enough.'

She waits while I find my feet and gather up my pack, then leads me to a pub she knows that will tolerate the likes of me. Inside it is dark and I can smell the Guinness slops, stale and bitter in my nostrils. 'I'd prefer a pint,' I tell her.

'You can fuck off,' she says, laughing. 'I offered you a coffee.'

'You can't blame a man for trying.'

'True.'

I sit in a dark corner, waiting while she orders. There is just one other customer, an old man sitting in the far corner with a pint of lager. Orange foam spills through a long diagonal slit in the red plastic upholstery beside him. He looks out the window at passers-by and lifts the glass to his lips, unaware of me. I hear Sheila share a joke with the barman, his deep chuckle mixing with her nervous squeak. The white sleeves of his shirt are rolled up past his elbows and his forearms are matted with black hair. I notice his hands, big, pink and soft looking, as he hands over the coffee cups, the teaspoons rattling. A television set with the sound turned down flickers dimly above the bar, abandoned.

Sheila puts the cups on the table between us and perches on a stool. 'Anything strange, Moses?'

'Nothing stranger than myself.'

She gives me a half smile and stares into her coffee cup.

'I get the feeling there's something you want to say to me, Sheila,' I say, disturbing her reverie.

'Yeah. There is, kind of.' She looks at me, unsure, then rushes on. 'Look, Moses, I've been thinking about your case a lot. Okay. Now, I don't mean to be offensive but I think there's a good chance that you've been in some kind of institution.'

I smile at her awkwardness, trying to put her at ease. 'Relax, I don't find that offensive.'

'Good.' She smiles back, surer now. 'I'd like to check into it, see what I can find out.'

'Thanks. I'd appreciate that.'

'You would?' She seems surprised, an eyebrow arching. 'I thought . . .'

'What? That I'd tell you to fuck off and mind your own business or something?'

'Yeah, something like that.' She looks down and begins to turn the coffee cup on its saucer, pushing the handle with her forefinger.

I lean towards her. 'Sheila, it's been killing me, not knowing. Waking up with images. A face, a name. Never enough to piece it all together. It's a bloody waking nightmare. You have no idea.'

'No.' She shifts on her stool. Her eyelids flutter and she looks back into my face, her expression serious. 'Moses, I have to warn you. You might not like whatever we find out.' As if I haven't thought of this. As if my every waking moment isn't filled with speculation. *Why can't I remember? There has to be a reason.*

'It can't be worse than this, Sheila. Nothing could be worse than this. I have to know.'

But doubts assail me, even as I speak. I want to know and yet . . . Shutters slam shut in my mind. Warnings. *No entry. Please keep off the grass.* My hands are folded on the table and she places one of hers gently on top of them, as if she sees me struggling, turmoil, and moves to quell the panic. 'I know, Moses. But I can't guarantee anything. I just don't want to disappoint you.'

'Life is full of disappointments,' I say, turning my hand in hers and holding it. 'Nothing ventured . . . Thank you, Sheila. Thank you for trying. Whatever happens.'

She smiles nervously and squeezes my hand. 'You're welcome, Moses. Any friend of Crunchy's . . .'

*

There are no guarantees. Sleep rough, live rough, rough. Occupational hazard for the homeless. He can't stop coughing. 'Me poor chest,' he says, spitting phlegm, racked again, pain written on his face. 'Me poor fuckin' chest.' It happens to people like Crunchy. Left out. There are always repercussions. The nurses take us seriously. They know Crunchy. Everyone knows Crunchy. He's a character. He's not faking. He doesn't have to fake it. If he was just here looking for a warm place to spend a few hours, they would turn a blind eye. After all, he's a character.

'You're all right now, Crunchy,' says a thickset girl with a country accent, bending over him. 'Sure what's a little cough to a lad like you?' But Crunchy is blue; he's finding it hard to catch his breath. He sucks in oxygen between bouts, his hands clutching at the front of his shirt, as if the weight of it is suffocating him. He leans against me, cupped in a plastic seat in the emergency room, shrivelled. She looks at me across his head and I can see that she is worried. 'I'll just get the doctor to have a look at you, Crunchy,' she says, her voice loud and jovial, at odds with the look on her face. 'Sure it'll make you feel important, won't it?' She pats his shoulder and moves away briskly, her flat shoes slapping on the tiled floor.

'Sweet Jaysus,' wheezes Crunchy when she's gone. 'Me fuckin' chest's on fire.'

I tuck his head under my chin, the way I would a child's, and pat his back. *There, there. Everything's okay now. Everything's . . .*

They admit him straight away. No messing. Pneumonia is dangerous for people like Crunchy. Sheila says that she will come at once, her voice sounding thin on the telephone. 'They won't tell me anything, Sheila. He looks awful. Christ.' I shouldn't be like this, snivelling like a baby.

'Relax, Moses. I'll be there as soon as I can.'

I hang up, returning Sheila's crumpled card to my pocket, and thank the nurse for letting me use the phone. 'Don't mention it,' she smiles, returning her attention to her clipboard.

*

'I'm arsed,' he tells me later, in the ward.

'No way.' He just glares at me. 'Sheila's on her way to see you.' I try to hold his hand but he pulls away from me.

'Fuck off, would you. What are you, a fuckin' homo?'

'Jesus, Crunchy.'

'What the fuck are you doing here anyway?' He pushes himself up in the bed. The effort makes him cough again. He looks weak, colourless.

'I . . .'

'I thought you said you were from Wexford.'

'Yeah? So?'

'Well, fuck off back to Wexford. Stop bothering me.' I stand up, confused, my mouth opening, but Crunchy takes my hand in his then and squeezes it. 'Good luck, Moses,' he says, his voice softer than I have heard it before. 'I hope you find what you're looking for.' I feel tears welling up in my eyes. Crunchy lets go of my hand, releases me. 'Now fuck off, you fucker.' He folds his arms and turns his face away from me.

II

It takes a week to walk to Wexford. Going home. I sit beneath a tree in Castlebridge, sheltering from showers, near enough to know that I will make it before nightfall. I wonder what I will find when I get there, what memories, released, will permeate my consciousness. Or will I just find hints, perhaps, tantalising clues to my ancestry?

If it takes a man a week to walk a fortnight, how many apples in a barrel of grapes?

I catch myself chanting it, over and over, riddle me this. And, because I am conscious of the words, they take on startling significance, beginning a deluge of images that floods through me.

An old man sits in a pub, cloth cap pulled tight on his head, his ears sticking out like butterfly wings, his cane leaning against his knee, his pint glass big in his bony hands. He raises a Guinness bottle and pours the dark liquid down the inside of the glass. His hands are shaking and the clinking of the bottle on the lip of the glass sounds like distant fairy bells. 'Come on now, Sprog,' he says to me, standing beside him, hardly taller than his knee. 'If it takes a man a week to walk a fortnight, how many apples in a barrel of grapes?'

'Three.'

'No. Wrong answer. I thought you were clever. Try again. If it takes . . .'

But every answer is wrong. My grandfather lifts me and settles me on a bony knee. He breathes hard from the exertion.

'I don't know the answer,' I tell him. *'How many apples are there, Grandad?'*

'Well,' he says, *'I can't tell you that. You have to work that out for yourself.'*

'Why?'

'Now, you see, when you're young you think you know everything but you don't. You have a lot to learn. And – do you know what? – when you're old, you still don't know everything. But you know enough to know that that's all right.'

He lets me taste his stout. The bitter aftertaste causes me to screw up my face and rub at my tongue with my fingernails. 'Yeuch.' The men around the table burst out laughing.

'Jaysus, Donal, he'll never make a drinker.'

'My round. Donal, same again?'

'Aye. Come on now, Sprog. If it takes a man . . .'

' . . . a week to walk a fortnight . . .' Another piece of the jigsaw falls together. My grandfather's name is Donal. I feel my brow wrinkle, a thought burning somewhere like a distant itch, just beyond my reach. I think of Crunchy. 'Don't try so hard, Moses,' I mutter to myself. The rain has eased. I stand up, ignoring the blisters on my feet. Hoisting my pack, I start the final three-mile walk to Wexford.

*

Coming home. I walked across the bridge that first day, the wind sucking the breath from me. *'Sure you're only a bit of a lad. You'll need stones in your pockets, walking across that bridge, or you'll blow away.'* Youth remembered, coming home. But only snatches still. Blue hair, a shrivelled face with ruby red lips. Lipstick. Kissing my cheek . . .

I stopped at the apex, shuddering, the rain, strong again,

stinging my face, my hair whipping at my eyes, beard bedraggled. I watched somebody jump from here once, on a calmer night than this. Strange. I remember it clearly, everything acute. He stood on the railing, facing us, his left hand wrapped around the lamp-post, the bottle flailing in his free hand. Cars stopped, adding to his audience. His anger camouflaged his words, slurred anyway from drink. Soliloquy.

We watched him weave and held our collective breath, morbid fascination holding us enthralled. Someone reached for him, '*Get down out of that, you gobshite,*' but he snatched his leg away, precarious for a moment. High wire. And we retreated. I wanted him to jump. Silently I urged him on. *Go on, show them. Show them how serious you are. Show them . . .* He stopped talking suddenly and the tension seemed to drain from him. His beard was matted, his long hair knotted and dirty. Froth gathered at the corners of his mouth. His teeth were yellow and broken. Peaceful, the anguish gone from him, he looked at us one by one, as if registering our existence for the first time. His eyes searching each and every face, taking us in. Like Jesus, sacrifice. *Sacred heart of . . .* We were his witnesses.

He turned, twisting slowly on his left leg and a hush fell across the crowd. His moment; I watched his fingers relax, saw him letting go. He toppled forward in silence, his arms outstretched, the bottle still clutched in his right hand. When we heard the splash the crowd erupted around me, people screaming, rushing forward, '*Someone call an ambulance . . .*'

I stood motionless amongst them, responsible. I wanted him to jump. Somehow it made sense. I understood his pain, even then. His outrage. I felt his fingers cold against the lamp-post, numb. His fingernails scratching on the smooth surface, the tenuous grip he had on life. I felt the demons struggling within him, the nonsense words escaping him, falling on deaf ears. *Help me.* And then the mind-blowing realisation. *There is no help here.* He searched us one by one. He tried to find a reason not to fall. We watched him submit, saw him plunge into the abyss. Secretly sated, we allowed our own demons to feed. Responsible.

They never found the body.

Now, clutching the same lamp-post, I wondered; if it was a different night, if the water stood motionless below me, like glass, and if I leaned forward just enough, would I see his body floating beneath the bridge, his arms folded across his chest and his hair billowing around him like a halo? Would he be my own reflection?

III

The streets here tantalise me, hiding secrets from me, teasing. I think each time I turn a corner that a truth will be revealed. But no. This narrow, crooked town guards its secrets jealously and well, its twin steeples standing like sentinels, unmoved.

I walked up Bride Street, towards the church, and fancied, for a moment, that a hand closed on mine. My mother's face came fleetingly and distant. Indistinct, I could not separate the features. And then, before my mind could take a hold of her, she disappeared again.

I don't know why I came here or what I expected. I don't know much of anything anymore. Except the children. The children could be mine. I saw her on the first morning, dropping them to school. I saw her profile, from underneath the cardboard, and something lurched sideways in me. Memory.

Our lips brush and I tremble at the dry softness of her. Hand on my chest, she tells me, 'Go to bed.' I lie awake all night and wonder if she's thinking of me too.

The children could be mine.

There is a yearning in me, a sense of something missing. They electrify me, current coursing through my veins when I watch them, feeding my obsession. My wife, my children. Skulking in doors and alleyways; clues, elusive, torture me. But there is solace in the knowledge that these children could be mine.

I know them now, these three. Facts gathered effortlessly, snatches of conversations eavesdropped. Gossip over shopping bags, a ragged man lies extraneous on the path. *Her husband left her, deserted her in Dublin . . . She's back living with her mammy now . . . It must have been another woman . . . Poor children, without a daddy . . .* Ignored, I am a shadow here, embarrassment best stepped over. I move outside the adult world, a cloud.

But minors are aware of me and taunt me when they see me shuffle, shoulders stooped, past school gates. Their prejudice is waiting to mature. Bravery is bred behind walls. There is safety in numbers. They have named me Johnny. *Want to buy a carpet. Penny for the baby. Johnny, Johnny, there's custard on your chin.* Another alias. Shuffle on regardless. If Crunchy was here he would rattle at the gates, spitting through the bars and pounding at them with expletives as a Christian Brother stood scowling on the top step, like a bat. He would run off cackling . . . If he was here. Are they so naïve? Does it not occur to them that I don't need to pass here every lunchtime? Their jeering reassures me. I know that I exist.

But these three are special. I watch their evolution. Over a fence, through a hedge. They are blow-ins, immigrant imps fresh from Dublin. Not from here, they will never fit, like shrunken shoes or someone else's underpants. They are different. Like me. They remain apart. Like me. They close ranks and cling to each other, brothers and sister, blood, sweat and tears. And me, I cling to them. Over a fence, through a hedge. We grow together.

Peter is tall for his age, but brooding. The absence of a father makes him frown. It's hard to be the man of the house when you're twelve. William is smaller and sweet but with a temper. Tantrums blow up fast, but wither without notice. Eleven is an awkward age for dark boys like William. And Grace is only seven, the baby. Everybody's pet. A small blond repetition of her mother, she has eyes to die for.

*

I must be careful. There are lots of weirdos about. A woman with a pram stood motionless on the Main Street, her foot frozen on the brake, watching me walk ten paces behind the children. Perhaps she noticed how my head was cocked, listening to their speech. Perhaps she just likes watching tramps. But I must be careful.

They would not understand. How could they? When I see the child, when her dark eyes find mine, suddenly I am a father again. A *father*. Like before. *One and one*. Logical. Like numbers falling into place. *I feel the weight of the infant in my hands, I see the crooked, toothless grin. The warmth of its hairless flesh against me, soft. The baby smell. My heart near spilling over.* And when the loose bond between us breaks, her turning away and rushing, laughing, to her brothers, I feel a tightness in my chest. I am nothing again. A husk. And later I will huddle somewhere, cold maybe, and I will feel the emptiness come gnawing at my belly. The craving will return. I need her. Need them. Family. To remind me I was whole. Once. *One and one*.

*

I kept my distance that first day, following them from school. Afraid of being noticed, knowing that conclusions would be drawn. It surprised me that I followed them regardless, impervious to seeming impropriety. *Dirty old man. Have a lollipop.* It wasn't like that, but I kept my distance anyway. Never out of sight, though, as if they had me on a string. Powerless, drawn, I skulked along behind, the inevitability comforting me. As if our paths were somehow intertwined. Me merely there by chance. Coincidence. Fate's puppet.

They walked ahead, oblivious, trading stories, kicking along in their school uniforms. *Who decides that children should wear grey?* It struck me as strange that they should get along so well and, for a moment, it occurred to me that I might be the victim of their spell. Conjured up, summoned to observe their coven. But then, what would that make me?

They crossed the bridge, me shadowing, a transient, unnoticed. Walking, perhaps, on the other side of the road, or pausing, pretending to tie a shoelace or rummage in my pack, when they stopped to throw stones into the mudbanks. Excited voices, high-pitched, led me on.

Their grandmother's house stood beside the river, where the estuary opened, a sprawling bungalow surrounded by trees and hedgerows. The door closing behind them seemed to break a spell. My senses, returning, brought more traces of memories. As if, by watching them, they plucked me from my morbid self-obsession, allowing me to breathe. The graveyard. An awareness that pieces of my past lay buried there.

I retraced my steps and passed through the gates, tombstones rising in front of me. A young man in a black suit leaned against a hearse, his legs crossed at the ankles. His left hand was buried in his pocket and a cigarette dangled from the loose fingers of his right. He watched me pass, his eyes following my progress, his head still. He lifted his arm as I drew level, took a drag on his cigarette and blew the smoke casually in my direction, his eyes cold. A knot of people gathered by a grave to my left, muttering. A priest shook holy water on them. I moved to the right, winding through the headstones, a path opening before me as if I knew where I was going. My mouth was dry, I could feel my tongue sticking to the roof of my mouth. The muscles in the backs of my legs quivered. I stopped beside a simple grave, my hand resting on the headstone, my head hanging.

I could feel the consciousness drain from me. 'Pull yourself together, Moses,' I whispered, concentrating. 'Come on, now. One and one.' I sat on the low wall next to his grave. Remembering. Calling him across. *'You can make it, Jimmy, you can make it.'* The train thundering down the line . . .

James Roche lived from 1965 to 1979 and is remembered by his loving parents and his younger brother Michael.

*

I am invisible. Light bends around me. Yes. That must be it. Misfit. Diseased. I am a leper, and my malady has led me to translucence. Incongruity has made me wispy, intangible. If I stood in their way on the Main Street, waving my arms and sticking out my tongue, vision impaired, people would pass, not noticing. Unacknowledged, I would remain, gesticulating in their wake. Mine is a strange power. Given. It springs from a collective desire for ignorance. If they do not see me, I do not exist. The world is safe. The world is normal. Comfortable. The cracks are painted over.

So I get closer to the children than I would have thought possible. Than I should be. At first I expect voices. *You there!* But vigilance is painful. Bad things only happen to other people. Caution is carcinogenic, acknowledgement would be an invitation. I will not touch. I only want to watch, to feed upon their energy. Passive participation. As if their lives can act as lifelines, reel me in. But the access I am permitted makes me angry. I could spirit them away. It would be easy and no one would be the wiser. The thought frightens me. That I can think it. That I could do it.

So I turn protector, watching over them. I follow them every day. Patient, I wait for them to pour from school, like a prison wife awaiting a release. I come to know their habits.

Dinner, eaten at the kitchen table, Peter sits nearest to the window, William to his right, Grace opposite. Their grandmother shakes their clothes out on the porch when they get home. In civvies they emerge and play until their mother swings her car into the driveway. They crowd around her then, hugging, welcoming her home. She ushers them inside, their homework pending.

I stand across the road, behind the hedge, shadows lengthening around me. Waves of jealousy and loss sweep over me. *I imagine evenings by the fireside with slippers and a newspaper. Or helping Grace with sums, Peter frowning, chewing on a pencil, William buried in a book. My wife's hand rests on my shoulder and I touch her pale skin, cold against my fingertips, hard bones brittle underneath. We are family. I am home.*

May. It is still cold when the sun goes down. I tug my coat around me and settle in for the evening. Later I will watch the house give way to sleep, lights extinguished, like eyes closing, until at last it looms above me, darkened. Prayers said, they are safe. I will stay awake. Watching, unacknowledged. I am invisible.

*

Each new thought threatens an avalanche. I see something that sparks a memory and another piece of me reveals itself. I remember father now, and hospitals. The sterile smell and waiting. My grandfather's arm around my shoulder, guilt eating at my innards. *I hope he dies.* Nurses looking at me pityingly. *Good boy.* Mistaken. 'I'm fifteen,' I want to tell them. 'I'm not a boy. I'm fifteen. And I'm not good. I hope my father dies.' But my grandfather's hand steadies me.

'Your son has had a stroke, Donal,' the doctor tells him, pencils in his breast pocket.

'Christ.' His face is ashen and his bony fingers tighten on my shoulder. 'Oh Christ.'

'It's too early to say how bad,' the doctor is saying. 'We'll have to wait and see. For now, all you can do is pray.'

'He'll be all right, Sprog,' my grandfather says when we are alone. He puts his hands on my shoulders and turns me towards him, his eyes, weak and watery, finding mine. 'Everything will be all right. We have to pray, Sprog. Say a prayer for your daddy. That's all that we can do.'

He hugs me then and I am glad that my face is buried in his shoulder. Otherwise my thoughts might be exposed. *Dear God, I hope my father dies.*

I think about my father now and wonder what kind of man I am.

*

I could walk up to her door. Simple. Knock and she may answer all my questions. *'You seem familiar, madam. Can you tell me who I am?'* Perhaps I am her husband, the deserter. Half-widow, she will wilt when she sees me, dropping the flowers she was cutting for a vase, her hands rising, covering the circle of her mouth, our engagement ring flashing in the streetlights. Will tears come when she sees this ghost? Or will she fish in her purse, dismissing me with loose change and platitudes?

I pause in the driveway, my hand resting on the gate. How could it go? A man must have his reasons . . .

'Your children are beautiful.'

. . . Perhaps she will just call the police.

But I know this woman. The knowledge plagues me. Vague memories stir like restless phantoms, cerebral vapour trails. We once meant something to each other. I have been in this house. A visitor? Welcome . . . Still I pause. Undecided. Look at me, my beard matted with dirt, clothes strung around me, holes in the knees of my trousers, exposed skin burned brown, thick hide, oak-matured.

A dog barks in the next garden and a light comes on. What would I say to these people? I have sacrificed my right to pleasant conversation. I turn to leave but a door opens behind me.

'What do you want?' Her mother stands in the doorway, neck craned, wondering.

'Can you spare a few pence, ma'am?' I turn my eyes down, deflecting my face from her. Humbled, I hold out a filthy hand.

Her nose wrinkles but she does not slam the door in my face. 'Wait,' she says and disappears from view. Seconds later she drops two pound coins into my extended palm. 'Don't drink that,' she says curtly.

'No, ma'am. I won't.'

Then she is gone, her features screaming as the door closes, *'Begone, you filthy vagabond.'*

There is no recognition there.

*

I see women carry bundles, sometimes, and I feel the jealousy burn in me. Sleepy heads fall against their shoulders and they lock their fingers together, like patchwork baby seats behind little legs. Soft breath warms their cheeks, sleep coming thick, heart beats synchronous. Their children hang from them, trusting, like growths, umbilical, as if, uncut, they are still one. Or child feels mother's fingers, gentle on its scalp through fine hair, and comforted and safe it slips away, like a high diver cutting water smoothly. Submerged, secure, confident of waking, it drifts, with mother's shoulder as a pillow.

A child once trusted me like that.

*

We spoke. It was innocuous, perhaps she moved along without another thought, but, Christ, it meant a lot to me. We spoke.

'Can I help you?'

She struggled with her shopping bags, balanced on one foot, searching in her purse to find the car keys. She looked at me and smiled. 'That's all right. Thank you. I can manage.'

She smiled again, warmer. As if she meant it. As if I was normal. A kind stranger passing by. Samaritan, not Johnny Forty-coats or something. Blond hair fell across her face and a key emerged as if by magic. She lifted a knee, shifting her balance, and a tin of beans spilled from a plastic bag and bounced on the pavement between us. I bent, picked it up, and held it out to her.

'Thank you.' She dropped the bags into the boot of her car and took the tin from me.

'My pleasure.' I could see her daughter in her, the same cheekbones, the deep, brown eyes . . . Narrowing. She might have spoken then, '*Aren't you . . .? Don't I . . .?*' Or maybe she was wondering why I still stood, empty hand extended towards her, mouth open, vacant, staring. I started to turn away.

'Wait . . . I . . .' Her voice caught me. I turned back to look at her, to look into those eyes again, expecting recognition maybe. A spark. A clue. But she was looking in her purse again, bent. Looking for an offering, like Mother. *Don't drink that.*

I wanted to shout at her. *Look at me, for Christ's sake. You know me. You must know me. I know you. Look at me.* Instead, I said, quietly, 'No. Thanks. I don't want your money.'

She looked puzzled, a frown crawling on to her made-up face. 'I'm sorry. I didn't mean . . .'

'I know. Forget it.' My voice sounded bitter in my own ears and I saw her frown deepen. What did I expect? Vagrant. What did I think she would see behind the filth and grime? Her husband? *Honey, I'm home. I didn't recognise you with your clothes on.* Infantile. I left her there, wrapped in her leather jacket and designer jeans.

*

When the disappointment fades I feel foolish. Her brown-eyed blondness tricked me, revealed my fractured sanity again. I wanted it to be that simple. Home. Welcomed to the bosom of my family, they would piece me back together and it would not take them long to make me whole. But there are great gaps in me, like canyons. Crevices forged deep in my soul.

And what of Caroline? Her dark brooding? I feel adulterous now. What kind of bigamist am I to have hidden her existence from myself? In my defence, I claim the need for somewhere to belong. Displaced, I came like liquid, prepared to fill the spaces left by him, their father. I wanted it to be that simple.

But I know things now. More about myself. The guilt feels comfortable, familiar. Not blond, though. Their mother comes from a different time, a passing childhood crush, perhaps, or adolescent fumbling. *There is an echo of a dark-skinned girl. My anchor? Her touch soothes me, restores my equilibrium.* Caroline is beautiful in white. She floats. Vows and rings are given. We giggle on the altar. *You may kiss . . .* I lift her veil and, simply, she is stunning. *Till death do us part.* There is a hard edge to my guilt. There are secrets that I struggle to remember.

*

When school ends in June we are released, like jailbreakers, making for the border. A mob. Screaming and careering we are let loose upon an unsuspecting summer afternoon, long days ahead already filled with endless possibilities. My heart beats faster, schoolbag belting at my back, I am propelled by thoughts of nothingness. The bicycle hums beneath me, thick tyres smooth on the tar, pushed to its limits. I am aware of the muscles in my legs, feet pumping the pedals. Adrenalin junkie. Faster. Onwards. Out. Tomorrow . . .

Of course I seek them out. The school lies empty, haunted only by the ghosts of children past. No lunchtime taunts to reassure me, no solace here. *Johnny, Johnny, there's custard on your chin.* Without them I become ethereal, a figment of my own imagination. The memory of her eyes burns me, moves me to find them. I am waiting in the morning, sleeping in a hedge across the road. They tumble from the house, all unconcerned. William punches at his brother's arm and Grace comes pushing in between them. I follow them all day, discreet, as far removed as possible. Watch them swimming in the river. Home for lunch then out again, sunburn creeping on to their shoulders and across their noses. Sometimes Peter stands, his head to one side, watching the other two, and it stirs a memory in me. A child apart, a foreigner. Or Grace falls and clutches at a skinned knee, crying, forgotten about quickly when a new diversion comes along. They are weary when I see them home, their heads hanging, exhausted from the intoxication of it all.

A pattern emerges. Summer stretches, startling under deep blue skies. Barefoot, the children hop from hot rocks on to cool grass, me marking time in the woods beside the river. Holidays. Screeches of laughter guide me to them, draw me, inexorably, to the midst of them. This becomes our ritual. Carefree, they roam the countryside, making camps along the riverbank, me watching over them, a self-styled guardian angel. This unaccustomed country makes it possible for them to start again, forgetting Father from time to time as the sun dances through the trees and shimmers on the surface of the river. Entranced, I allow them to lead me, my amnesia hiding like a whisper in the gods.

Peter breaks a branch and fashions a bow, the smaller children gathering straight sticks for arrows. He ties a piece of string to an arrow and shoots it over a branch hanging above the river, the twine arcing in the sunlight, like a fishing line. They tie a rope to the other end of the twine and hoist it over the branch. A slip-knot is carefully constructed and pulled tight. They have a swing. Their industry rewarded, they sweep above the river, pendulous, propelling themselves, soaring at tangents, free-falling to the water amid whoops and screams and silvery cascades of foaming liquid.

They trudge home each evening in the fading light, reluctant, mother calling them across the fields. I watch them from the edge of the wood, listening to their legs rustling in the cornfield. *Same time tomorrow, same time tomorrow . . .*

But this is no perversion, though I know well that it could be so misinterpreted. I am Daddy, father protector. *Pater*, nothing more. Yet I feel a need to justify, explain. To me, if no one else. Mothering instinct. How could that be so natural if this is so perverse? Fathering instinct. Why not? They arouse such deep emotions in me, filling spaces, caverns in my consciousness. If they threw their arms around me it would not be a new sensation. Of this I am sure. I know the feel of fragile arms, like twigs. Weak bear hugs, sapping sapling strength. Flesh of my flesh. If I sleep at night now, which is by no means certain, I see a new face.

My child. Different. Mixed with hers. Grace. They have merged in my mind somehow. As if he . . .

I know now that she is not mine. Another chose to desert her, desert them, not me. But I am here, deserted too. And that binds us. Surely. As if he . . .

There is a promise at the end of every tired day. There will be another. Something to look forward to, watch them grow a little more tomorrow. Each ending promises a beginning. Nothing severed. Nothing final. As if he . . .

. . . As if *I* have been given a second chance.

*

Caroline lies naked in our bedroom, her belly stretched, distended. Her breasts are swollen, heavy, undiscovered. I lie beside her and she takes me in her arms, clasping my head to her bosom. She runs her fingers through my hair and traces my spine with long fingernails. I shiver. Eyes closed, the warmth of her. I can feel soft kisses on my hair.

'Are you afraid, my love?'

'Yes.'

'What are you afraid of?'

'I don't know what kind of father I will be.'

'Nobody ever knows.'

Her hands move on me. Velvet. The texture of her. Teacher . . . I don't know what kind of father I am.

IV

Jason is an interloper, fly-by-night, come recently to disturb our equilibrium. Little comfort can be found in his appearance. Miniature and stocky, he is a pale caricature of a child. In short, a runt. Hidden, I watch them contemplating swimming in the river, Jason running on the bank, flat-footed and floppy-limbed, his belly a white balloon strung to a pile of whittled sticks. Carrot top, he jumps high, whooping, descending, plunging, arse first, arms wrapped around his knees, sending plumes of icy water to suck the breath from tentative explorers at the edge. He emerges, freckle-faced and gap-toothed, grinning at the others. 'I told yez to get in quick.'

'We don't splash,' declares Grace, stamping a foot, her features cloudy.

'Splash this.' Jason, treading water, flips a finger up and bleats laughter; then sets his face and doggy-paddles to the rope trailing from the overhanging branch. He hauls himself out of the water, lips pressed together, breath held, red-faced exertion. 'Look at me.' He flails his legs, trying to gain some momentum. 'I'm Tarzan the ape.'

He is rougher than them, a country child, hard compared to cissy city slickers. They hesitate on the river bank, huddled in their swimsuits, uncertain in the sunlight. He revels in their fear of him, dominating and intimidating them. Small, he has never been taken seriously before, has never had the chance to be the leader.

Grace turns to Peter, her eyes brimming with tears, her pale chin trembling. 'I don't like him,' she says quietly. 'Make him go away.'

But Peter can just shrug his shoulders and look dejectedly above his siblings' heads at Jason dangling upside down above the murky water.

*

Playthings. Sticks are swords, turned sinister in Jason's hands. He needs to know how far he can push it. William sucks his skinned knuckles, where Jason's sword flew past the nailed-on hand guard, stinging, blood seeping to the surface. Belligerent, he fixes his opponent with a baleful glare; beaten, bloodied, never bowed. They are fast becoming enemies.

*

The siblings sit in session, uneasy, afraid he will appear and catch them scheming. I crouch in the copsewood, remote but still a part of it.

'He frightens me,' says Grace. 'He's too rough.'

'But what can we do?' William turns to Peter, his face bundled, pocked with question marks.

'You know what Mammy said.' Peter frowns, wrinkles already appearing on his young brow. 'We have to make friends here.'

'Not him.' William shakes his head, pouting.

'Well then we should ignore him.'

Grace begins to cry. 'I want to go home.'

'Okay, Gracie,' says Peter, 'we'll take you home in a minute.'

'No. Home to Dublin. To Daddy.'

The two boys pick at hangnails, bite lower lips, and bow their heads. I skulk in the undergrowth, impotent.

*

'How do you know when you're in love?' Jason hugs himself, jigging up and down, eager to reveal the punchline, his hyperactivity threatening to swallow him. The others stare at him blankly. 'Come on,' he shouts. 'Are yez stupid or what? How do you know when you're in love?'

'We don't know,' says Peter.

'Your girlfriend taps you on the bum and says, "You're in, love."'

Jason squawks with laughter and rolls over on his side while the others stare blankly at each other. I hate him for trying to curtail their innocence.

He stirs dark thoughts in me, this stunted child. Ruffian. I fester. He is a malignancy, his tendrils reaching into us, threatening to destroy us. 'He's just a child,' I tell myself, over and over before I sleep. 'Just a child. Perhaps tomorrow he will not come.' But I know that he will be there, spoiling. Disturbing them, robbing their exuberance. Proud father, surrogate, how can I stand by? I must.

*

The boys are swimming further up the river when he comes. Grace makes river tea and mud pies, her golden hair tied up in pigtails. Humming to herself, she is unaware of him approaching.

'Where's the other two?' His question makes her jump.

'Go away,' she says. 'We don't want you.'

'Shut up, you little cow,' he says, cuffing her across the ear, bringing tears to her eyes.

She stands up, determined, face scrunched up, staring at him. Only inches between them. 'I said get lost.'

'Women,' says Jason with exaggerated exasperation. 'Dad says they're only good for one thing. Shaggin'.' He throws his arms around her, pinning her arms to her side, rubbing himself against her and laughing hysterically at her screams.

Concern grows in me but I am reluctant to reveal my hiding place, lurking in the shadows behind a tree. It is only when he steps back and pulls his stubby erection from his swimsuit that I start to move.

'Suck this,' he shouts, leering at the screaming girl.

But Grace is there before me. She bends and plucks a nettle from the ground, thrusting it into the boy's crotch. His turn to scream, he wheels away, his hands wrapped around himself, twitching and hopping, his reflexes and the burning in his groin pulling him in a grotesque dance.

'Good for you, Gracie,' I whisper to myself, relaxing.

The boy speaks harsh words, like orange pits spit at her, his face a hateful grimace. I continue to watch from behind the tree, convinced now that this thing has run its course. I can see her shoulders shaking. He raises his hand, as if to strike away a cur. Small hand, fingers folded flush against the palm. A fist . . .

I hate you. I hate you, Daddy.' My son's fists hammer at me, like flies landing on my chest.

'Stop it, Donal.' I catch him by the wrists and start to shake him, my temper spilling over . . .

Her brothers come, attracted by her screams. Bantam champions, they wrestle him to the ground. They tussle. There is a moment. I could step out. *Stop that. Behave yourselves, you pups.* But I lose it, the way I lose most things. A fist finds a nose, draws blood. William rolls away, crying, clutching at his face. I watch this through a haze. I have begun remembering again. The most important piece . . .

I had a son. I know that now. I see his face, contorted, colour rising, 'I hate you . . . '

Peter and Jason still roll together, wrestling. William stands by furiously, blood spilling across his mouth and chin, staining his bare chest. I see him lift the rock, I sense what he will do but I am rooted to the spot . . .

My son. Where is my son? Where is Donal? . . .

Jason pulls free from Peter and climbs to his knees, crying now, snot running down his upper lip.

'Fuckers,' he screams, 'yez're nothin' but fuckers.'

The rock catches him across the temple, William swinging from behind. I hear a sound like eggshells being trampled underfoot. The child's face goes blank, shock registering in his eyes, and he tumbles sideways and slides into the river . . .

A policeman stands in my grandfather's doorway, asking if I'm in. 'We have some questions for your grandson, Mr Marlowe. It's about the boy.' My grandfather stands aside and points them towards the living-room.

'They want to talk to you about Donal,' he tells me in the kitchen. 'Go and talk to them.'

I shuffle towards another inquisition, my sanity in tatters, numb from lack of sleep . . .

Peter slides down the bank after Jason, landing heavily, up to his knees in water, casting around for the boy. 'You killed him, William,' he bellows at his brother. 'I think you fucking killed him.'

William stands silent on the bank, his hair still wet from swimming, his small white body quivering from the cold and shock. Grace takes her brother's hand and leans her head against his arm. He looks at her, tears rolling down his cheeks. 'I'm sorry.' I can read his lips across the clearing . . .

'We are mindful of your loss, sir. But questions must be asked . . . '

Jason explodes from the river, like a deep-sea diver lunging for the surface. The children scream and I am jerked back to reality. The boy sucks hungry breaths deep into starved lungs and flails about, a foot or two from Peter. The side of his head is bleeding heavily, dark liquid running down his neck and across his shoulder. 'You're all fucked,' he shouts between sobs. 'When I tell me da you'll all end up in jail. You're all fucked, yez bastards.'

They look at one another, family three, close, unspoken, a decision is reached. Peter reaches for the boy...

I lie strapped to a bed. Caged. A doctor smiles and slides a needle smoothly through my skin. I feel the tension slip from me, his voice, booming, echoing through darkness. 'It's all right now. You'll be looked after here. Just get some sleep, I've given you something to help you relax...'

Blood billows in the water, like a rumour, spreading... *I heard that he was kidnapped by a cult...* Peter holds the boy's head underneath the water, sobbing, salt tears stinging at his eyes. After-image, William lifts the rock and strikes. Burned forever on his retina. And mine. No going back now. He feels slick fingers wound around his wrists, crimson. Weaker now. Slipping. Like the boy's last breath. Escaping. Leaving his lungs. Given up to bubble to the surface.

Frantic thrashing stops. Suddenly. The boy surrenders. White foam dissipates, sliding, like his life, away, to mingle with the weeds along the river's edge.

Then Peter lifts his face and sees me watching from behind the tree. Our eyes meet. The other children follow his gaze and I am drawn to them. By them. As if their coven has some kind of hold on me.

'You saw,' says Peter, emerging from the river, 'that makes you part of it.'

I hold his gaze, displaced somehow, disturbed by otherworldly memories, alarmed by my inaction. It is as if I am sleepwalking.

'Do you hear me?' The boy is shouting at me now, red-faced, trembling chin, tears of shock coming. He pounds at my chest with balled fists. Spittle flies from the corners of his mouth. 'You're part of it. You have to help us.' I catch his wrists and start to push him away from me but he collapses against me, deflated, the fight suddenly drained from him. 'You have to help us,' he says again, quietly, his words forcing their way through sobs. 'You have to help yourself . . . '

'You have to help yourself.' A nurse's aide in a white coat proffers pills. He bends over me in a bright, sunlit dayroom, patches of blue visible above his shoulders through a large bay window. The walls are painted cheerful pink and dotted with colourful posters of flowers. 'Come on, now, take them. Good man.' His voice comes soft, soothing.

I see my own hands through a tunnel, reaching for the plastic cup. I see his teeth, smiling, and they somehow seem ferocious. His beard is black and thick, with two white streaks either side of his chin. The patients call him Dracula. I take the cup of pills in my trembling fingers and raise it to my lips. Take this cup and . . . No. I raise my hand and watch the smile freezing on his face, then hurl the contents of the cup to the floor, small, round tablets scurrying like beetles in every direction, skipping and sliding under tables and chairs.

'No.' Mine is a controlled anger, my voice calm, determined. 'I've had enough. I want my life back. Keep your fucking tablets.'

He sighs, bends, and starts to gather my debris. 'Suit yourself,' he says quietly, stretching to reach a blue capsule. 'I'm getting tired of this. It's the third time this week. We call you Moses in the staffroom, you know. Always throwing down your tablets.' He straightens and returns my sullen stare. 'It's your funeral,

Brandon. Personally, I don't give a shit any more.'

He leaves me sitting alone, my hands clasped in my lap, as if in prayer. This is where I begin my trip through the wilderness.

'You have to help yourself . . . '

Brandon. My name is Brandon Marlowe.

Donals

I

She will make contact with him now and they will be reunited. Reconciled through adversity, their animosity forgotten. There are bigger fish to fry. He will come from Dublin to the scene of the crime and there will be tearful scenes on her mother's patio. Perhaps they will kiss and make up, and he will run his adulterous fingers through her thick, blond hair. She will rest her head on his shoulder and sob quietly. 'My babies,' she will whisper hoarsely in his ear. 'The bastard has my babies.' He will pat her back and comfort her. 'There, there.' And all will be forgiven.

*

My grandfather is waiting, a sprightly eighty-four, the first time he meets his namesake. I hand the boy to him, drowsy from the journey.

'Come here, Sprog,' he says, his hands outstretched.

'You used to call me that.'

'Aye.' He smiles. His great-grandson wipes at an eye with the back of his hand, a lip hanging, and stares sullenly into Donal Marlowe's face.

'This is Donal, too,' I tell my son, my hand resting gently on his head. His hair is soft and fine against my palm. My grandfather balances him on a hip, his frailty forgotten. 'You can call him Grandad, like me.'

'You're very quiet, Sprog,' says my grandfather, pinching at a red cheek. 'What's the matter? Has the cat got your tongue?'

'Don't worry,' I say with a smile. 'The shyness won't last long. Enjoy it while it lasts.'

The taxi driver helps me move our baggage into the hallway. Paid, he touches his cap, and backs down the path, grateful for the tip. *'Goodnight, sir.'*

My grandfather leads me to the living-room. Donal, still balanced on his hip, eyes him suspiciously. He seems older than my memories of him. Four years since my last visit. He is greyer, his skin lined and weathered. Still thin, his back straight, he moves cautiously, one foot carefully placed flat on the ground before the other follows, as if the soles of his shoes will not bend. His hand is splayed against my son's back, overcautious, reluctant to trust himself with something so precious and fragile. I look at the back of his neck as he leads me down the corridor. Tufts of grey hair poke from beneath his collar. His head is extended, proud, like an aged gazelle. I think of him when I was young, old even then, but limber. He used to weed the flowerbeds without bending his knees. *'I was always fit,'* he told me once. *'That's why I'm so skinny.'* As a young man he played hurling for the county. He is still remembered for his vital goal against Kilkenny in the dying moments of a Leinster final. From two points down to victory; they carried him, a hero, from the field . . .

The living-room is warm. 'Good one, Grandad,' I say, nodding towards the fire. He smiles, grunting his acknowledgement, and sits in his usual armchair, Donal on his knee.

It is his art form, fire-lighting. We joked about it endlessly when I lived with him before. *'Demarcation,'* he would say, all mock indignation, if he caught me stoking it. *'If you want to help, go and get some slack in, boy.'*

On my return, he would kneel in front of the fire with a milk bottle full of water in his hand, the coal scuttle settled on newspaper beside him. He would carefully pour water

122

into each shovel full of slack, measured. Then, lovingly, he would plaster the black mixture on to the hot coals, like a bricklayer, patting the mound flat with the back of his shovel. The resulting hot, black slope would cook for an eternity and I would sit complaining of the cold until, eventually, orange cracks would begin to appear and captive heat would belch into the room. Afterwards, we would bask for hours in the furnace glow, watching dark landslides, and my grandfather would turn to me and snigger. 'Is that warm enough for you?'

Sweating in my shirtsleeves, I would answer from the corner of my mouth. '*Feck off, you old fart.*'

My son sits on his knee now and twists to look at me, uncertain. I nod to him and sit opposite. 'Go on, I say. Call him Grandad. Try it, he doesn't bite.'

'Grandad?' Donal looks curiously at the old man.

'That's me,' my grandfather says, smiling. 'Well, it's close enough. Isn't it, Brandon?'

'Yeah. It is.'

'You're going to come and live with me for a while,' he tells his great-grandson. 'You and your daddy. I think we're going to be great friends. Would you like that?'

Donal looks to me again, frowning. 'It's all right, Donal,' I tell him. 'Everything is all right.' But the child looks precarious and close to tears. I cross the room and take him from my grandfather. 'He's just tired,' I say. Donal puts his thumb in his mouth and buries his head in my shoulder.

*

By teatime he is warming. His face cracks into a smile when Grandad calls him Sprog. It is his first boiled egg, and the toasted soldiers fascinate him. My grandfather dips a soldier into the orange egg yoke, a demonstration. He transfers the soggy soldier quickly to his mouth, egg yoke running down his chin. 'Oh Jaysus,' he exclaims, 'that's hot. You'd want to blow on that, Sprog.' Donal shrieks with laughter as the old man fans his face and crosses his eyes, blowing futilely.

'Grandad is silly,' he tells me.

After tea I can see that he is struggling to stay awake. He doesn't want to miss anything. 'Come on, Donal. Time for bed.'

'I want to say goodnight to Rita.' I can see the colour rising in his cheeks. Flustered, he looks around, frightened by the sudden unfamiliarity. 'Where's Rita?'

She answers on the second ring, her voice soft. I hesitate, familiar feelings surfacing, fresh wounds opened. 'Hi. It's me,' I tell her. There is silence on the line. 'Donal wanted to say goodnight.'

'Hi . . . Yeah . . . Okay . . . Put him on.'

Donal grins and chats to her, answering questions gleefully. *'My ears hurt on the hairy-plane. We were on a train. Grandad is funny. Daddy is okay but he was sad earlier . . .'*

I picture her sitting in her flat, dressed for work perhaps, smooth legs crossed. Her face softens as she listens to his voice, the receiver pressed to her ear. Maybe she will start to cry and black mascara will mix with teardrops, leaving dark streaks on her cheek. *'Goodnight, Donal. Be good. Do what your daddy tells you. Yes. Of course we're still friends. I love you too. Goodnight.'*

When he says goodnight for the third time, I take the phone from Donal. 'Rita? Are you still there?'

'Yes, Brandon. Still here.'

'I . . . He misses you already.'

'I miss him.'

'Rita . . . I wish . . . I don't know what to say.'

'There's nothing *to* say, Brandon. Goodnight.'

'Yeah. Goodnight.' My voice is heavy with emotion. When I turn around my grandfather is standing in the living-room doorway watching me, his hands on Donal's shoulders. Donal is leaning back against his legs.

'All right, Brandon?'

'Yeah. All right. Come on, Donal, it's time you brushed your teeth.' I take my son's hand and lead him up the stairs.

*

Donal slept with me in my old room. I put him to bed early that first night and stood in the doorway watching him, tiny in my single bed, curled and breathing deeply, his thumb still in his mouth.

My grandfather handed me a whiskey when I came downstairs. 'He went off okay, then?'

'Out like a light. Poor little fecker is exhausted.' I raised my glass to him. 'Cheers.'

'*Sláinte.*'

'You're looking well, Grandad. How have you been keeping?'

'Sure, struggling, but there's no use in complaining.'

The fire spat and crackled beside him. He filled his pipe and lit it, the sweet-scented smoke drifting across the room to me. I remembered standing close to him as a child, the smell of stale sweat and tobacco in his clothes and hair, the nicotine stains on his fingers. He used to be a forty-a-day man before he took up the pipe.

'Are you back for good, Brandon?'

'I don't know . . . Yeah. Maybe. Yes. I think it's best for Donal.'

'Aye.' He sucked on his pipe, deep in thought, wondering, perhaps, how far to push. 'Have you heard from his mammy at all?'

'No.' I closed that avenue sharply. I saw his eyes narrow slightly.

'Do you want to tell me about Rita?'

'She's . . . Look, I really don't want to talk about it now if that's all right . . . I will. In time. Just not now. Okay?'

'It's okay, Brandon. I don't mean to be nosy.' He looked away from me into the fire.

'I know, Grandad. Look, I should have kept in touch better . . . I shouldn't . . . It's not fair of me, just turning up like this.'

'You're here now, Brandon, and you're welcome.' He looked back at me across the room, smiling. 'You and the Sprog. I'm just glad to have you here. I've missed you.'

'I've missed you too, Grandad.' I could feel myself softening, believing, finally, that I was home.

My grandfather's grin widened around his pipe and he nodded towards the door. 'He's a cute one, though. Isn't he?'

'Oh yeah.' I smiled back at him, thoughts of Donal warming me.

'The spit of you.'

'He has Caroline's eyes.'

'He does.'

We sat grinning at each other, both drifting through private thoughts, easier with each other now. After a while my grandfather took his pipe from his mouth and leaned towards me, stretching to put a hand on my knee. 'It's good to see you, Brandon,' he said, his eyes bright.

When I went to bed Donal was like a hot-water bottle, curled amid the blankets. I pushed him towards the wall and climbed in beside him. He stirred, grumbling, turned towards me and settled back to sleep, his hand resting against my chest. I hugged him to me and kissed his forehead.

'Goodnight, little man,' I whispered. 'Everything is going to be okay.' But my heart was heavy and my thoughts kept returning to Rita, alone on the streets of Frankfurt. Deserted.

*

The first time, when my mother died, he took us in, father and son. There were no question marks. *The boy needs a family.* My father, drunken, needed all his energy to mourn her. No room for me. At ten I could not make it on my own. I felt the absences engulf me. Powerless, I welcomed the cold embrace of illness, retreating to the isolation of my inner rooms. My father's father resuscitated his grandson gently but with a patient firmness that permitted no digression. He would not let me linger for too long in dangerous culs-de-sac.

Little wonder, then, that I should flee to him two decades later. He listened with the same solemn poise that had teased out my survival when my mother's death had threatened to destroy me. I told him about my friend, about his dolorous existence. Outcast, he had clung to us until his heart stopped beating. Gerald's death cast me adrift again. *'I don't want to die alone, Grandad.'*

He watched me calmly, his pipe, unlit, turning slowly between his fingers. 'We all die alone, Brandon,' he said at last. 'It's how we live that matters.'

I grew conscious of my sleeping son upstairs and wondered if my father had occupied this chair so many years before. What tears were shed while I succumbed to weary slumber? Had he pondered his own mortality, like me? What words were passed between them? And later, after the stroke, when he bathed his son and wiped the spittle off his chin while feeding him, did Donal Marlowe wonder at the cycles of his life? Did he curse the disappointments? A wife who died in childbirth, a son roughened by a life without a mother. Mistakes. And now the need to do it all again. Did he question his recurring penance as he changed soiled bed linen, rolling his unresponsive son aside?

'It's how we live . . . ' Another cycle. He did not hesitate. He welcomed us with open arms, another damaged father and son. More refugees, descendants needing mending. No question marks. *The boy needs a family.* 'Come here, Sprog.'

It seemed his house was built for men, and three men occupied it once again.

II

It was hard at first to work again but Matty Devlin was good to give me my old job back. We had known each other since we were kids. Even then, overweight, he had airs and graces. His clothes were always immaculate, creases you could cut yourself on. He had the luxury of knowing that he would get his father's fuel and haulage business. We used to call him Slick.

My father, on the other hand, was a gravedigger. 'At least you'll have no problem getting a plot,' Matty would say at every opportunity, winking and nudging others into laughter. *Slick.*

I hated him and envied him but when I qualified I went to him, not really knowing where else to turn. I had watched my grandfather weaken during my years at university. My father was too much for him, a burden that he could no longer bear alone. He argued when I told him. *'You have to make your own life, boy.'* But even his objections were infirm. He knew he needed help. My father was a heavy man and age had sapped the strength from Donal Marlowe. I had no choice. I had to return to Wexford. And jobs were far from plentiful.

I turned up one Monday afternoon with my degree folded neatly in my suit pocket. 'Who's dead?' said Matty, roaring with laughter. 'You look like you've been to a funeral.'

'How are you, Matty?' I smiled, stretching a hand out. He shook it without standing up.

'I'm fantastic,' he boomed. 'Never been better. How the hell are you?'

'Good. I just got my degree.'

'Well good for you!' he said. 'You won't be going into the family business then.' He roared with laughter again and then became suddenly serious, sitting back in his chair to study me. 'What can I do for you, Marlowe?'

He looked like a baby elephant behind the desk, his soft hands folded in front of him, resting on his gut. His face was mottled red and shiny, as if he had been scrubbing it with steel wool before I arrived. The jacket of his tailored suit was draped across the back of his chair and he wore red braces and a matching tie. I noticed his gold cufflinks, heavy against the white sleeves of his shirt. Still Slick, I thought.

'I need a job, Matty,' I said. 'I'm not fully qualified yet, there are still exams I have to do. But I'm good, and if you need a cheap accountant . . .'

He thought for a moment, clicking a fingernail against his front teeth and looking at me. 'All right,' he said. 'Why not?' He laughed and put his feet up on his desk, lacing his fingers behind his head and balancing his chair on two legs. 'You've caught me in a good humour and I need someone to do the books. Office manager, let's say. When can you start?'

That easy. But fifty pounds a week into my hand was a pittance even then. 'If you don't like it you can lump it,' laughed Matty, and I bit my tongue and stayed. It was better than the dole and Matty let me write my own job description and even gave me study leave. I told myself that it would look good on my CV.

It was harder the second time. He scowled at me when I entered his office. The years had not been kind to either of us. I wore a sports coat, borrowed from my grandfather. It was too tight across the shoulders and added to my discomfort. Matty looked grey and tired. His fingernails were dirty and the top button of his shirt would not close against his fleshy neck. I could see a black ring around his collar. He leaned heavily on his desk, double chinned and already balding. His teeth were bad and I could smell his halitosis from across the room. He looked up at me from under heavy eyebrows, waiting.

'The girl said . . .' I looked back over my shoulder, gesturing with my forefinger.

'What do you want, Marlowe? I'm busy,' he said.

'I'm looking for work, Matty.'

'Do I look like I give a shit?' He fiddled with a wedding ring as he spoke, moving it back and forth on a fat finger. His voice was a low growl.

'Come on, Matty. This is hard enough. I have a kid. Give me a break, will you?'

He snorted. 'Don't talk to me about hard, Marlowe. You're not the only one with problems. I have a demanding wife, two snotty little bitches for daughters and an ulcer. So you give me a fucking break.' He sighed and pulled his ring off, spinning it on the desk in front of him. He put an elbow on a pile of papers, buried his fist in a jowl and looked at me, his lips pursed. I stood looking back at him, silent. 'All right,' he said at last. 'You used to be a mate and you're a good accountant. I'll find something in the office for you, but I can't afford to pay much.'

'Thanks, Matty.' I could feel my mouth widen into a smile. I was light-headed with relief. 'I owe you.'

'Yeah, yeah. Right,' he said. He continued to spin the ring, more interested in it than in me. 'Now fuck off and leave me alone. Jacinta will take your number. I'll call you in a couple of days when I sort something out.' He hoisted himself on to one buttock and farted as I left the office.

On the way home I stopped at a corner shop and bought

some sweets for Donal and tobacco for my grandfather. As I pocketed my change it struck me that I had come full circle. I was back where I started. No. Not quite. Years ago there had been hope. Working for Matty Devlin had been a beginning then. There were weekends in Dublin with Caroline, plans to be made. I remembered my first pay cheque, the caravan we hired in Curracloe, the mixture of guilt and giddiness as we undressed each other in the sand dunes, and, when our hearts stopped racing, the comfort of each other's arms.

This time my hope was gone.

*

I find myself shivering by the fire, a blanket wrapped around me. It is not the first episode that I have had since my return. I feel the snapping, like a rubber band breaking, and suddenly my consciousness cuts through me; seeping, piercing, like a hot ejaculation. I am aware of what has gone before. Vague, as if I have been stranded in a parallel dimension. I have seen shadows lumbering, heard voices or the sound of my own breathing. Slow. Laboured. Loud. Time has passed but I cannot say how much. I blink and take a deep breath, looking up.

'They called for you from work.' My grandfather sips tea in his usual position. He has seen this before.

'What did you tell them?'

'The usual. That you were sick. Matty Devlin is no eejit, though, Brandon. He knows your history.'

'Everybody does. It's a small town.' I rub my face. No bristle. It has not been long this time, thank God.

'Are you all right?'

'Yeah. Thanks. Donal?'

'He's asleep. It's after ten.'

I do not take to changes any more. I need a pattern to survive. Milestones. Step by step. If I look beyond tomorrow I am lost. Like fear of heights, if I focus on horizons I am safe. Unaware, I can skirt around the edge of the abyss.

'I'm sorry, Grandad.'

'It's not your fault, boy. You're all right now.'

He raises the mug to his lips again. It seems large, surrounded by his thin fingers. His sleeves are rolled up past the elbows and the silver hair on his forearms looks like networks of frost on fragile branches. For ten years he cared for his invalid son, teaching him to talk a second time. I stood outside the door some nights and listened to his patience. *Again, Francis. Come on now. Say it again. Rich blood, poor blood, ten times fast.* For ten years he watched his boy unravel, working the dead half to preserve the muscle tone. Appearances. It must be hard to survive your own child. Now me. When he finds me unresponsive he compensates. Feeds me. Clothes me. Kisses my son goodnight and searches for explanations. *'It's not your fault, Donal. It's just that Daddy isn't well. It's nobody's fault.'*

I need to find a system. I need to find a pattern to survive.

*

'You're separated, aren't you, Brandon?' Jacinta asked from beside the kettle. She wore short skirts and flirted with all the drivers but I had been off-limits since I started working there, as if she didn't know quite what to make of my brooding presence. Her sudden interest made me feel uncomfortable. 'Sugar?' She held a cup up, pointing at it with a painted fingernail.

'No. Thanks. Black.' It was the first time in almost five months there that she had made coffee for me.

'You are, though?'

'What?'

'Separated.' She carried two cups across the office and sat on the edge of my desk, crossing her slender legs, her knee almost touching my arm.

'My wife lives in Dublin,' I said, evasive, taking the cup from her. I could feel the colour rising in my cheeks and my scalp tingled from the proximity of her attention.

'Your son lives with you, doesn't he?'

'Yes.'

'So, how come he doesn't live with his mammy?'

Perhaps it was an innocent question, asked without agenda, but it made my blood run cold. It was a question best avoided and one that I had previously ignored. I had become accustomed to sudden silences when I met my grandfather in the pub, the pint glasses poised in mid-air, hanging like half-finished sentences when I entered. As if there was something unnatural about a boy being left solely in his father's care. I did not acknowledge their discomfort. I passed amongst them, preternatural parent, single, single-minded, singled out. I was, at least, an oddity.

'He lives with me,' I said abruptly.

'Oh I'm sorry, love,' she said, resting her hand on my shoulder, her face softening. *Love. She must have been ten years younger than me.* 'I didn't mean to pry. Don't mind me.'

'It's okay. It's just . . . Look, I shouldn't have snapped at you.' Her sudden interest in my personal life had unsettled me.

'It's only, well, we don't really know each other, like.' She put her cup down, uncrossed her legs and stuck her hands underneath her thighs. She started to swing her feet back and forth beneath the desk, like a schoolgirl. 'We've been working together for, like, ages and we've never had a chat.

134

I don't really know anything about you, only that you're an old friend of Devil's . . . oh shit.' She retrieved a hand and put it to her mouth, giggling. 'I mean Mr Devlin. You won't tell him, will you?' She looked worried suddenly and her feet stopped moving. I smiled at her.

'No. Of course not.' I had not noticed before how pretty she was. She had a thin face with high cheekbones and her skin was alabaster pale and smooth. Her black hair fell shoulder length and looked thin and impossibly silky. *I thought of my fingers wound there, a thumb resting against the curve of her ear.* Her small breasts stood firm and proud beneath her orange jumper and she had a wide black belt pulled tight around her slender waist. She crossed her legs again and, for a brief moment, my eyes dropped and I saw the top of her black stocking and the soft pale flesh on the inside of her thigh. I looked away quickly and she tugged her skirt down. 'Devil,' I said, to break the silence. 'So that's what you call poor Matty.'

'Everybody does,' she said. 'Like, the lads in the yard and all. It's not just me.'

'No?'

'No!' She thumped my shoulder with her fist. 'Don't go getting me into trouble, you.'

'I wouldn't dream of it.'

'Not half.' She giggled again and leaned towards me and I could smell her perfume. 'You're not so bad, you know,' she said. 'A little serious, like, but you're okay. You should come for a drink with me and the lads after work sometime.'

'Thanks,' I said. 'I might just do that.'

I watched her walk across the office, swaying on her high heels, her slender buttocks moulded against her skirt. When she got to her desk she smiled back across the room at me, knowing that I had been watching her walk, aware of the power she had. She was playing with me, teasing, and I knew it. I'm too old for that, too tired, I thought. I knew that I would not go drinking with her. I was far too fragile for her game.

*

He turned four in July, his first party without Gerald. Grandad and I tried to make amends. He is growing fast, sometimes surprising us. His baby curls have straightened in our time here and baby talk is non-existent now. A fierce intelligence burns in him. It frightens me, his need to know. He will start school in September. We picked a bag for him last week, with new pencils and a pencil case. He already reads, I've started him on Enid Blyton.

'Dad,' he says one night after dinner, his brow furrowed, 'I think you're sick sometimes because you miss Rita.'

I pause and look at him over my newspaper. He is kneeling in front of the fire with a toy car in his hand. 'What makes you say that, Sprog?'

'Grandad says sometimes we have to leave you alone. He says that you're not well and no one knows why.'

'Come here, wee man,' I say, folding my newspaper on my lap and beckoning him over. I can hear my grandfather washing dishes in the kitchen, plates clinking.

'I think it's because you miss Rita,' Donal is saying. 'You were never sick when we lived with her.'

'Thank you, Einstein,' I say softly, hooking a leg around him and putting my hand flat on his stomach. 'You could be right.'

'I think I am,' he says, his head on one side, his hand resting on my leg, 'because sometimes when I think about her I feel really, really sad too.'

'I'm sorry, Sprog,' I tell him. 'I know you miss her just as much as I do.'

III

I do not expect her parents to tell me where she is but Donal needs a mother. I pause with my hand on the doorbell, considering. *Nothing ventured* . . . I hear the notes sound deep inside the house and an inner door opens almost immediately. A rectangle of light falls across the hallway and a television set can be heard in the background. Footsteps clatter on the floorboards and a shadow grows in the stained glass of the front door. When she opens the door I am lost for words. My face must mirror hers, the shock. Her mouth opens and she covers it with a hand. White, she takes a step backwards into the hallway.

'Caroline . . .'

'Oh Jesus. Brando. I'm sorry . . . I just wasn't expecting . . . Sorry . . .'

Inside, her stepfather turns off the television and shakes my hand, his grip firm. 'Brandon,' he says. 'It's good to see you again.' As if I am a boyfriend, coming to collect his stepdaughter for a trip to the pictures on a Saturday night.

Her mother perches on the edge of the sofa, trying to hide her discomfort. She keeps smiling at me, a nervous tick in the muscles of her left cheek and her eyelids fluttering wildly. The redness of her lipstick makes me think of open sores. 'Tea,' she says suddenly, springing to her feet, as if the perfect excuse has just occurred to her. 'I'll make a pot of tea. Come, David.' Her husband follows her from the room.

When the door swings closed we look at each other and

laugh. 'Christ,' says Caroline. 'It's the first time I've ever seen my mother stuck for words. It's almost worth it all for that.'

'You look well, Caroline.' The smile freezes on her face and suddenly she looks self-conscious. She is dressed casually, jeans and a light blouse. Her hair has grown again, a dark bob, and she has gained a little weight on her face. She has always been inclined to plumpness and I cannot help but think of her weight on me, the solidness of her against me.

'Thank you. You too. I'm . . . Brando, it's so strange to see you. Sorry. It's a shock. I don't know what to say.'

'You could ask about your son.'

'Of course. I'm sorry. How is . . . ?'

'Donal. I called him Donal.'

She smiles sadly at that. 'After your grandfather,' she says. 'I like that. He was a nice man.'

'He still is. We're living with him now.'

'Oh.'

There is a tap on the door and her mother leans into the room. 'Do you take sugar, Brandon? I'm sorry. I don't remember.'

'No. No thank you.'

'Cup or a mug?'

'A mug,' I say, not really caring.

'And will you have a biscuit or something . . .'

'Mother,' says Caroline angrily.

'All right, all right,' says her mother. 'I'm going. It won't be long.' She bows out, apologetically.

'Doesn't take her long to recover, does it?' says Caroline and we laugh again, strained. There is a silence then and I shift uncomfortably in my seat. She stands beside the fireplace, chewing at her lower lip.

'How is he? Donal I mean.' Almost as if she is afraid to

ask, as if she has given up the right. 'I think about him often. And you.'

'He's beautiful, Caroline. Perfect. He has your eyes.'

She smiles at that but the smile fades quickly and her brow furrows. Like Donal. There are so many similarities. 'He's four now,' she whispers, almost to herself, her dark eyes turning towards the fire, reflecting the glowing coals.

'Yes.'

'It doesn't seem like four years.'

'I . . .'

A silence falls between us again. I hear her stepfather's voice raised in the kitchen:

'Leave them alone, for Christ's sake.'

'I'm only bringing them tea.' Her mother pleads innocence.

'They don't want any bloody tea, Mona. Stay out of it.'

Caroline looks at me through soft tears.

'So, this is where you've been?' I say lightly, trying to break the awkwardness.

'No.' She laughs and rubs an eye, half turning towards me. 'That's what makes it so strange. I'm visiting tonight. That's all. Another night I wouldn't have . . .' The thought remains unfinished.

'Fate, then.'

'Yes. It must be.' She smiles at me again, uncertainly.

'I didn't think they'd tell me where you were,' I say. 'Thought I might have to beat it out of your mother.'

She snorts with laughter at that. 'You and whose army?'

'A formidable lady.'

'I'll say.'

'Why didn't you call or write or something?' The suddenness of the question startles her. She looks at me as if I've slapped her. 'I mean . . . Four years, Caroline. Without a word. Why?'

'I . . . I just couldn't.'

'I loved you, Caroline.'

'I know . . . But . . . Jesus.' She puts her fist to her mouth and bites at a knuckle. This time the tears flow freely. 'Why did you have to come here now, Brando? After all this time? I was ready to get on with my life again.'

'Donal needs a mother.'

'So find him one,' she snaps. 'My mother found a father for me.'

'He needs you, Caroline.'

'No. He doesn't. I don't want a child. I don't . . .' She stops and puts a hand on the mantelpiece, her face angled away from me. She is struggling to control herself. She pinches her nose between her thumb and forefinger, sniffing. 'This is way too emotional.' Her voice is calm again now. 'I'm sorry, Brando. This can't be easy for you either. Let's start again. Okay?'

'Okay.'

She sits on the couch beside me, perched, like her mother, so that she is facing me. 'How long have you been home?'

'About six months now.'

'And how are you? Really.'

'Better. A lot better now. I'm in control most of the time.'

'Good. I'm glad, Brando.' She stretches a hand towards me and touches my cheek lightly with her fingertips. 'I used to worry about you so much . . .'

'I know.'

'Why did you come back, Brando? I'm surprised. I thought you loved Germany.'

'I did. I do. It's just that . . . Well, I thought that Donal should be Irish. You know? We always said we'd want our children to be brought up in Ireland. He's starting school soon, so it seemed like the right time. That and . . . Caroline, Gerald died last Christmas.'

'Oh Lord.' She begins to cry again, her hand falling away from me. 'Gerald. I'm so sorry to hear that.'

'He was good to us. To me and Donal. He was Donal's godfather, you know. It meant a lot to him . . . To both of us . . . He . . . Christ, I miss him.'

She is staring into the fire, remembering her friend. Her thoughts, perhaps, on coffee mornings. 'He promised me he would look after you. Did you know that?'

'No.'

'He told me not to leave. He said that I would regret it for the rest of my life.' She shivers and sits upright. 'He was right, Brando. I will. But that doesn't change anything.'

'I don't suppose it does.'

She catches my hand in hers now, tender. Fond. 'It's good to see you, Brando. It may sound strange, coming from me, but I did miss you. I wish that I could make you understand.'

'You don't need to, Caroline. What's done is done . . .'

'Am I forgiven?' She squeezes my hand.

'If you come to see him.'

'Oh, Brando. I don't know.' She sniffs, close to tears again.

'Just think about it, Caroline. That's all I'm asking. Here.' I hand her a slip of paper. 'I've written down my number and the address, in case . . . Write or call me when you decide. Okay? I won't ask more than that. You should come, though, Caroline. You owe it to yourself. It would do your heart good to see him. He's so . . . special. He's so like you.'

When I stand to go she stands awkwardly beside me, not knowing what to do. A handshake would be silly and hugs and kisses are dangerous. 'Tell your mother I'll take a rain check on the tea,' I say, 'but thanks.'

She smiles, her hands pushed into the back pockets of her jeans. Before she has time to feel self-conscious I lean over and give her a peck on the cheek. 'Goodbye, Caroline.

I'll show myself out.' I turn then and leave quickly.

Her stepfather catches me at the gate. 'Brandon. Wait.' I stop and turn towards him. 'I know it's none of my business,' he says conspiratorially, his face close to mine. *We are all men here.* 'But when my daughter came back from Germany she was in pieces. It has taken us a long time to help her through it.' He puts an arm around my shoulders, walking with me towards the bus stop. 'Now, Brandon, I'll say this only once.' I feel his hand tighten on my shoulder. 'Don't ever set foot on my property again.' He stands back then and looks at me, his eyes icy.

'You're right,' I say, smiling at him. 'It's none of your fucking business.' I walk away from him then, not looking back, but I can feel his cold stare on the back of my head the whole way down the street.

*

She has not called before his first school day. I hide my disappointment, dressing him. He looks comical, half dressed and serious, his belly sticking out. 'Give me your arm,' I say, holding out his shirt.

'I can dress myself, Dad,' he says, scowling.

'I know, I know. Just humour me.'

'You know that you're going to be late for work?'

'They can wait, okay?'

'Okay.' He lets me button up his shirt.

'I'm proud of you, Donal.'

'Why?' he asks, exasperated. 'Every kid has to go to school.'

'Wise guy.' I pinch his shoulder and he giggles and twists away from me. 'Sometimes you're too smart for your own good. Do you know that?'

'So you say.'

'I love you, you little varmint. Do you know *that*?'

'Yeah.' He falls against me, laughing, and I hug him for a long time.

*

We fall into a rhythm as the year stretches. Golden brown, we could be content. I am present more than not now. The comfortable familiarity of my grandfather's house, once accepted, stabilises me. And my son enjoys his new life. School presents challenges and allies. I thought that he would come home crying on that first day, not wanting to return. But my fears were groundless. I left work early to be there when he returned. He bounced into the kitchen, his schoolbag on his back, and words could not come fast enough. Stories and descriptions tripped off his tongue like furious hailstones. I watched him jigging up and down and smiled, happy that I had made the right decision. He is Irish.

At the end of October my grandfather strings apples in the living-room and spreads newspapers on the floor. Donal and I dunk for coins and monkey-nuts in a basin full of water, my grandfather sitting by the fire with his pipe in his mouth and a towel across his lap, waiting to dry his great-grandson. *'I can't believe your auld Da never had a Halloween party for you before.'* Donal emerges from underneath the towel, his hair all tossed, pointing and making his naughty face. *'Watch it you, you scallywag.'* We dress him up for trick-or-treat and take him to the neighbours. Candy for a baby. Later he is too excited to sleep and I read him stories until after midnight.

Still she does not call . . .

One Sunday in November I cannot get out of bed. Donal fetches my grandfather. He puts his hand on my forehead and asks how I am feeling. Worms writhe behind my eyeballs. 'You have a fever,' he tells me. 'I'll move the boy into the other room. It's time he had his own room anyway.'

I have kept him with me for my own sake, to comfort me. His sleeping presence soothes me when darkness closes in around me. I watch him breathing in the soft glow of the night-light until, reassured, I slip away to sleep. Because of him the nightmares keep their distance. But now a fever fills me and I drift between waking and sleeping. Tangled in the storm-strewn sheets I mutter to myself in desperation, or to faces floating free in my delirium. Defenceless, I am taunted by complexities. Appellant. There are circuits left to close.

. . . I wake. It must be early afternoon. Pale light penetrates the blackness of my burning sleep. A dream, it's just a dream. Rita crying quietly, her head on Gerald's shoulder. Horst watches me, his eyes burning, and Gerald turns his face away. We are standing over Donal's broken body. A dream, it's just a dream. My consciousness recoils from the unthinkable and yet, subconsciously and lingering, I remain accused. And when I close my eyes the image is still burned there. I am guilty. I know what I have done. I know that I have killed him . . .

That night I hear my grandfather put the child to bed. 'Daddy's sick. You have to sleep in here. You don't want to get the flu, do you?' The boy cries himself to sleep in the room next to mine. It seems that I have been comforting him too.

In the morning, after Donal leaves for school, my grandfather calls the office. His voice comes angry through the open door. Protector. 'No. It's not like that,' I hear him telling Matty. 'It's just the flu. I've called the doctor . . .' It seems that I am not to be depended on.

Doctor Benson shuffles into my room at midday. His stethoscope is cold against my back. *Breathe.* He prescribes an antibiotic. 'Are you on any other kind of medication?' he asks, scribbling his signature.

'No.'

'Well you should be. I remember you . . .' My past is catching up with me.

Still she does not call . . .

*

Horst still writes. Envelopes come with German postmarks and his spider scrawl. He is well, he says, and thinks of Donal often. Donal sits on my knee when I read the letters to him. He listens carefully, his head cocked to one side, his lips pursed. He smiles when Horst tells him how Frau Fischer swept the leaves up off the front path, but when the wind caught them and they blew all over it again she had to start from scratch. Accomplices, they used to watch her from the window in autumn, their heads close together, giggling, crouched down so that they would not be seen. *What memories do you have, my son? Can you forgive me for my weakness? I should, at least, have given you stability.*

At first there are notes from Rita, too, and I hold the paper close against my face and breath her subtle perfume. Stung, I read the desperation in her words: *She is struggling without us. Horst cannot bring himself to talk about it but she knows he feels the same. The picture of a horse that Donal drew for him is pinned to the back of his kitchen door. He cried when he found it folded in my letter . . .*

The thread between us is perishing, my longing for her

deadened now. Sometimes I find myself thinking of her as if she is a character in some book that I have read. I have forgotten what it feels like to touch her, the warmth of her kisses . . . My memory has blocked her out, as if the pain of remembering would be unbearable. Choices have been made and I must live with them. For Donal . . .

'My life is harder now,' she tells me in her last letter. 'I could survive before, alone. But having you and Donal somehow softened me. I am different now. You raised my expectations. Dearest Brandon, should I dare to dream?'

But dreams are dangerous. Sometimes they are too easy to believe, even when they are built on flights of fancy. I could not lie to her . . . I told her in September about finding Caroline. Her letters stopped.

Horst still writes but now the envelopes are just addressed to Donal.

*

It is Christmas Eve when she comes. A year now since Gerald died. I am recovering, new skin thickening. Old wounds lie dormant underneath. Donal jumps to his feet and runs into the hallway when he hears the doorbell ring, perhaps expecting presents. I hear my grandfather's footsteps as he makes his way from the kitchen. He pauses in the doorway, looking at me kneeling in a tangle of Christmas lights. He is wiping his hands in a dishcloth. 'Has Santa's little helper deserted you?' he says. 'Don't worry, I'll get it.'

I can hear Donal's voice, excited. 'Who is it, Grandad?'

'We won't know until I open the door, now, will we? Step back, Sprog. Watch yourself.'

I hear the door swing open, feel the cold draught sprint along the corridor and curl around my knees. I hear faint murmuring, a woman's voice. 'He's inside,' I hear my grandfather say, his tone grave, the humour gone from his voice. Curious, I stand up, trailing tinsel and fairy lights.

'Will you show me where he is?' I recognise her voice, singsong, talking to the child. They appear in the doorway, Donal holding her hand.

'This lady says she wants to see you, Dad,' he says.

'Hello, Caroline.'

'Brando.'

She is wearing a long, mauve coat, buttoned up over black, stockinged legs. Her scarf is still wrapped around her neck but she holds her gloves in her free left hand. Her cheeks are red from the cold and her eyes are watery. She sniffs and hesitates, still holding Donal's hand. My grandfather appears in the doorway behind her bearing brightly wrapped boxes and a face like thunder. He puts the boxes on the hallstand.

'Come in,' I say, mobilised. 'You must be freezing. Sit over by the fire. Grandad, take her coat.'

'No.' She half turns to him, resisting. 'I . . . I can't stay. Daddy is waiting in the car. Look, I just . . . Well, I brought some presents. Happy Christmas, Brando.'

'Caroline. You've come this far . . .'

She puts her fingers to her lips and swallows hard, blinking back tears. Donal looks up at her confused. 'Come on, Sprog,' says my grandfather, reaching for him.

'No.' Donal's head snaps around at the fierceness of my voice and my grandfather pulls his hand back as if stung. I walk over to my son and squat beside him, putting my hands on his shoulders and looking steadily into his eyes. He looks back at me, worried, his brow forming its usual furrow. 'Relax, wee man,' I say, smiling at him. I put my hand on his head and run a thumb across his forehead. 'You'll give yourself wrinkles. Stop worrying. It's good. Good news. A

147

really nice Christmas present.' I look up at Caroline and she nods, crying openly now, but smiling too. 'This is your mammy, Donal,' I say. 'This is Caroline. Your mammy.'

Donal wrinkles his nose and peers up at her. 'Do you want to help us decorate the tree?'

IV

January is filled with good intentions. We are resolute. New Year. Intact, we emerge from a Yuletide dreamscape, grimly determined, and attempt to put our world to rights. Willpower wanes, however, as the year grows. Cold weather weakens our resolve. Already brittle, our conviction shatters in the slow course of shrunken days, fumbled by chilblained fingers. It seems that imperfection is resilient.

I thought that we could start again. Family. I dreamed of kissing her at midnight on New Year's Eve, her Adam. Naïve, then. Still. My grandfather tried to warn me between the years; a peculiar Irish trait, born of a nation's cynicism. *You must keep your expectations low.* Experience perhaps . . .

For a time it seemed as though it could work. She fell in love with Donal straight away. He sat playing at her feet while my grandfather poured whiskey for her stepfather, and I saw him lean against her, his hand curving across the floor with a toy car. He looked up to gauge her reaction but she did not publicly acknowledge him. Her cheek reddened slightly and I watched her raise her glass to her mouth to hide a half-smile. Then I noticed her knee bend slightly as she applied a little pressure to his back with her shin. He smiled, returning his attention to the car, and kept his back against her. Conspirators, secret warmth passed between them and no one was the wiser.

They are like bookends, their dark eyes dominating oval faces. Like angels, they float somehow and I grow more conscious every day of my mortality. Her hand finds his face, sometimes, and their skin seems to melt together, like pale liquid. As if they are still joined. Umbilical, they have found each other again.

'I want to take him to Dublin,' she tells me on her third visit. 'You know. To meet my mother.'

'Can't your mother come here?'

'She doesn't like to travel.'

And, when he goes with her, the weekend seems to last forever.

'Aren't you coming, Dad?' he asks as we pack his suitcase.

'No, Sprog. I've got things to do.'

'Oh. Okay.'

Fickle little bastard! I am jealous. I think, maybe, I am losing him.

*

Maybe I should kiss her. There is mistletoe about.

*

She begins to come for weekends, booking into a guesthouse in Selskar. My grandfather tells her she is stupid; there is plenty of room for her at the house but she declines his invitation, preferring to maintain her independence. *'Bloody waste of money,'* he mutters to himself on his way to the kitchen. *'I'll put the kettle on.'* We develop our routine and I find myself awaiting Friday nights.

She drops her bags at the guesthouse and then comes here for dinner. Donal, scrubbed, waits up for her, dressed in his pyjamas and dressing gown, a teddy on his lap, short legs jutting out beyond the cushion on the armchair. He is wearing orange slippers. 'How long till Caroline gets here?' he asks over and over until my grandfather loses patience and scowls around his newspaper. 'Hould your whisht, Sprog, will you? Go help your daddy with the dinner.'

We are chopping carrots when the doorbell rings and Donal clambers off his high stool in the kitchen and runs to the door, his teddy trailing. He is hopping up and down when I get there. 'Relax, kiddo, I tell him,' winking and trailing my hand through his hair. 'You should never appear too eager to a lady.' I swing the door open, my hand still resting on his head.

'Hey, guys!' Caroline is laden with presents. 'How's it going?' She hands me a bottle of wine and lets me kiss her cheek before she bends to take him in her arms. 'So tell me about your week,' she says to him, carrying him down the corridor. Giddy, he strews wrapping paper in his wake. I follow, picking up the pieces.

Later, when Donal is asleep, we sit in the kitchen sipping wine. I can hear the television in the living-room. My grandfather is watching the *Late Late Show*. The candle has burned down and is flickering between us. Dishes are piled in the shadows on the sideboard.

'He's beautiful,' she says, swirling the red liquid in her glass, her eyes far away.

'Like his mother.'

A puzzled look creeps across her face but she dismisses it, replacing it with a half-smile. 'He's smart. God. You have to watch yourself around him.'

'Ain't that the truth? The little fecker would buy and sell you.'

Her lips are dark and moist in the candlelight and the flame creates a golden fire in her eyes. I remember nights with her in Germany, in the early days, when we pulled the mattress off the bed and dragged it to the living-room, candles lighting everywhere. Wrapped in sheets we leaned against each other, listening to Mozart on the stereo and drinking wine until, thick from the alcohol, we made muffled love and fell asleep in each other's arms.

'It's good to see you, Caroline,' I say. 'I . . .'

But something in my voice seems to frighten her. 'Don't,' she says, her forehead puckering. 'Please, Brando. Don't.'

'Don't what?' There is anger in my voice.

'Just stop.'

She gets up and switches on the light. Stark, electric whiteness washes over everything, dousing my reverie. I am delusional no longer.

'We have to do the washing up,' she says, her back to me, moving dishes to the sink.

'Caroline, I . . .'

'Leave it, Brando.' When she turns to me her eyes are on fire.

'No.' I feel my temper rising. 'We need to talk, Caroline. Where is this going?'

'Nowhere. *This* is going nowhere,' she says. She has rolled her sleeves up and her hands are wet and dripping on the floor. 'You wanted me to meet my son. I did, I love him, and I'm grateful. But that's it, Brando. Nothing more.'

'And us?'

'Oh Brando. There is no us.' There is a frustrated gentleness about her. Her shoulders sag towards me and she wipes at her chin with the back of a damp wrist. 'Don't you get it?' When I don't respond she sighs and sits in the chair beside mine. 'I'm coming here for him, Brando. That's all. I'm sorry if I gave you any other . . .' She takes my hand and leans her head against mine. 'Jesus, Brando.' I can feel her breath soft against my neck. 'I'm so sorry. I never wanted to hurt you.'

But I can only sit in silence and blink back hot tears. The emptiness is threatening to swallow me again.

*

I have begun my descent, aware of the futility of trying to maintain my elevation. I was a good man once. Or were the images I conjured of myself a mere illusion? Fanciful? I have always done what's best for Donal, I tell myself. At least there's that. I would do anything for the boy. Anything . . .

But now he needs a father to depend on, and I am not dependable. Matty told me in March. It snowed on St Patrick's Day. It's not unheard of. I remember once before, when I was six or seven, when it snowed this late in the year. I was in the Cub Scouts and I woke up early that morning, excited about marching in my first parade. Mother dressed me in my uniform, a smile playing on her lips, her pride clumsily hidden. I followed her downstairs, stretching for the banister, moving loosely, like a marionette, and peering down the length of my body, past navy jumper, shorts and socks at black, shined shoes. My cap felt snug on my head and my free hand smoothed the neckerchief against my chest. But when she opened the curtains in the kitchen my heart sank. Dazzled, my thoughts did not turn to snowball fights and snowmen. She looked over her shoulder at me, biting her lower lip, her hand still wound around the curtain. Later, I held her hand as we walked to Mass. I had refused to change and wore a long coat over my uniform. I sat beside her in the friary and watched my bare knees turn from red to purple, stinging in the changing temperature. She patted my hand when the friar announced that the parade had been cancelled due to adverse weather conditions. I bit my lip and hid my disappointment but she knew.

Matty cupped a match and lit a cigarette, drawing the smoke deep into his lungs. 'They say these things will kill me,' he grunted, shaking out the match and dropping it in

153

the snow at his feet. 'I've been smoking forty a day for the past ten years, but no luck so far.' He curled his lip and took another drag. Snowflakes settled on his black overcoat. His eyes were red-rimmed and watery and he wore a bobble hat pulled down around his ears. 'This fuckin' flu might do the trick, though. I feel like shite warmed up.'

'What can I do for you, Matty? Why did you want me to come in on a holiday?'

We stood outside, surrounded by idle lorries. Mounds of coal lay sheltered under green tarpaulins, undisturbed as snow fell everywhere. 'I love it here when it's quiet and the snow comes,' Matty said, staring across the yard, snowflakes resting on his eyelashes, like dandruff. 'It's so . . . different. You know . . . the way the blackness just gives way. Sort of gradual, like, and everything gets soft . . .' He looked at me, his eyes bright, and flicked ash off the end of his cigarette with his thumbnail. 'Cleansing,' he said, his teeth yellow in the pale sunshine. 'That's the word. Cleansing.'

He looked back across the yard again and started humming to himself. I stood quietly beside him, my hands buried in my pockets.

'Matty,' I said at last. 'Is there a point to this?'

He jumped, as if he had forgotten that I was there, then turned back to me and put a heavy arm across my shoulder. He looked steadily into my eyes. 'We've known each other a long time, Marlowe, haven't we?' I nodded, frowning. His face was close to mine and his breath smelled like an old ashtray mixed with alcohol and Silvermints. I knew that he kept a whiskey bottle in the bottom drawer of his desk. He was usually drunk by midday and, most nights, he did not get home until well after closing time. 'Maybe that's why this is so hard,' he said. His eyes slipped out of focus and his jaw slackened, as if I had suddenly become transparent and he was studying his own death notice, posted on a wall behind me. 'Or maybe I'm just getting soft . . .'

'What is it, Matty?'

He seemed to snap back to the present. 'I have to let you go, Marlowe. I'm sorry.' He took his arm off my shoulder and put his hand in his pocket, his eyes never leaving mine. I stood there with my mouth open. 'It's nothing personal,' he said.

'Oh Jesus, Matty. You can't . . .'

'Oh come off it, Marlowe. Don't act all hurt innocence. You know full well I have no choice. If you weren't a mate I would have let you go weeks ago. You hardly ever turn up anymore and when you do you're worse than useless. You're . . .'

'My son, Matty. What will I tell my son?'

'I told you before, Marlowe,' he snapped. 'You're not the only one with problems.' He took a hip flask from his pocket, unscrewed the lid, and took a swig. When he offered it to me I shook my head and he shrugged, fastened the flask, and put it back in his pocket. 'My wife is screwing some randy little fucker from Tagoat,' he growled. 'How do you think that makes me feel? Life isn't fair, Marlowe. It's one kick in the bollox after another. Did no one ever tell you that?' He rubbed his hand across his face and leaned close to me, his voice softening. 'Look, I'm sorry, all right? But I'm trying to run a business, for Christ's sake.' He pulled an envelope out of an inside pocket. 'Here,' he said, holding it out to me. 'Two weeks' severance. I'm sorry, Brandon.'

I stared at him until he looked away. 'Keep it,' I spat, and turned on my heel. I got to the gate before he caught me, his hand heavy on my shoulder.

'Marlowe, for fuck's sake. Stop acting the prick, will you?' He was panting, his massive bulk sagging after the run across the yard. He wiped at his nose with the back of his hand

and sweat rolled down his forehead. 'Look,' he said, 'I have a fucking fever. I should be at home in my bed. I don't have the energy to argue with you. Just take the fucking money, you gobshite.' He pushed the envelope into my hand.

I felt the fight drain from me. My shoulders slumped and I put the envelope into my pocket. 'I'm sorry, Matty,' I said. 'I understand. Look . . . thanks.'

'What would you do, Marlowe? If you were in my shoes, what would you do?' He looked as if he was about to cry. 'I mean, I need someone I can depend on. I can't depend on you, Marlowe. I just can't depend on you.'

'I know, Matty. Like I said, I understand.'

. . . I have begun my descent. Free fall.

*

Sometimes, alone, the frustration chokes me. I feel my fingers curling into fists and veins bulging. When I open my mouth to scream there is no sound and, whimpering, I fall back on my bed and sob dryly, biting on the quilt and almost gagging. There is no end to this it seems. I am afraid for my consciousness. It is as if my essence has been ruptured and, molten, my identity streams unchecked from every pore. Leaking away. I must stop this. *Christ. Jesus. Listen.* But I don't know what to ask for. Is it too late to learn to pray? I dig my nails into my palms and sit rigid on the edge of the bed, holding my breath, my teeth clenched, straining until I almost feel a popping in my temples. *I have to get a grip.*

Donal will be waiting downstairs, breakfast almost done. I will walk to school with him and crouch to kiss him at the schoolyard gate. My son will run to a knot of children by the steps and, breathlessly and effortlessly, melt into the laughing, screaming, touching, pushing mob. Careless, they begin another day. Forgotten, I will watch him for a moment until, obsolete,

I turn and head for home. Unknown to him . . .

How can I tell the child? He worries already and he is only four. A child should not worry. Not like that. So, I lie. *'I've worked it out,' I tell him. 'I start work later now and finish early so that I can spend more time with you.'* I have not got the heart to tell him that his father is a failure. What will he think when he is older? Role model? Jesus. I am growing more and more detached. I cannot cope. *I'll show you how not to do it, son.*

Francis Marlowe would laugh at me if he were still alive. He would blow smoke into my face and cough fine foam on to his frozen chin. His live eye would twinkle and the cigarette would burn between two upturned fingers of his good hand. 'Now, you little fucker,' he would say. 'Suddenly you're not so judgemental any more. Fallen off our perch, have we?' And he would laugh until he doubled over in another fit of coughing, emerging, eventually, with the twisted grin still plastered on his face. 'Don't feel so bad,' he would mock me. 'It was your mother's fault. She's the one who gave you airs and graces.'

Even from the grave I feel his ghost come hovering above me on the darkest nights. Sleepless, I toss and turn below him, fancying I feel his cold breath foul upon my cheek, his hollow laughter ringing in my brain. *'It isn't easy to be a father,' I whisper in the blackness. 'We can neither of us change what we are, so rest in peace.'*

'You must tell the boy,' my grandfather tells me icily. 'Your subterfuge is pitiful.' But fear of obsolescence has stolen my initiative. My son has made a liar of me. I am bound now and cannot be less than what he thinks of me. 'I don't know who you are, Brandon.' My grandfather's lip curls and I know that my stubborn passivity turns his stomach. He has recognised my weakness. It seems that I am letting everybody down.

I am at my lowest point. In trigonometry I'm sure there is a name for me. Or astronomy. Aphelion? I stood in the bathroom tonight looking at my reflection in the mirror, wondering how I became this, how all the possibilities eroded, creating this: the sum, less than all the parts. Accountant, expatriate, husband, father . . . Child. My yellow shirt and grey, knitted waistcoat disguise my insecurity, the transience of my nature. Chameleon, I have tried to make it all work, tried to be what is expected. I see the red-rimmed eyes, the weariness skulking deep within the pupils. I hold secrets deep. Hidden even from me. Nine-fifteen. I brush my teeth and say goodnight to Grandad. '*The* Pat Kenny Show *is starting soon.*' My leave-taking is a major dis-appointment. Stay, boy, his eyes say. This is as good as it gets. Two old farts together . . . Haven't you noticed, Grandad? I go to bed earlier and earlier these days. Sleep is an escape for me. Tomorrow comes quicker. And then that too can slip by. Fast. Early to bed. Tomorrow. Past. I want this life to end but cannot end it. Live it fast. Sleep through it. The coward's way out. I wish . . . I wish my life away.

Caroline took Donal walking today. I watched them from the kitchen window, hidden behind the blinds. They walked hand in hand, their heads bent towards each other, deep in conversation, and I realised my own dispensability. She laughed and bent to kiss him and he twisted in her grasp, his face turning towards me. Joy. Christ! The love in his twisted features shot holes through me. I felt my heart plummet. Fuck. Plummet. That's the word. How did it feel? A father finds out that he is not necessary. Work it out. I am one inch tall now, in my yellow shirt and grey, knitted waistcoat. I put them on for her, really. But she is here because of our son. Donal. It's all about them now. I am . . . superfluous.

'What do you want from me, Caroline?' I ask her in the hallway after kissing Donal goodnight.

'Nothing.' She seems confused, unsure of what I'm asking. As if I've thrown a curve-ball out of left field and she's wondering how to deal with it. She wants nothing from me but threatens to take everything. 'I'm sorry. I don't know what you're asking.'

'Christ.'

'Keep your voice down, Brando.' The words come hissed at me, a terse whisper, as if unspoken accusations lie concealed within the moment. 'Donal.' It is an explanation for everything.

'Fuck it.' I turn and stamp down the stairs, my fists clenched. I want to hit something, as if the violence would help. Walls seems inappropriately unyielding.

'Brando,' she is at my shoulder. 'Calm down. Are you okay?'

'No.' Hot tears sting but I blink them back. I have my pride. At least that. My pride. 'Of course I'm not all right. I know what's happening. I know . . . Oh for fuck's sake.'

'What? What do you think is happening?'

'I'm losing him . . .' Out. I catch her wrist, squeezing. *For Christ's sake understand . . .* She looks frightened, as if I could hurt her. As if I could hurt either of them. As if she doesn't understand how much I love them.

'Let go of me, Brando.' Her voice is small but defiant.

'Caroline. I . . .' She pulls her arm away.

'You're mad,' she says, her voice raised, outraged. 'I thought . . . No. You're mad.'

'I won't let this happen. I won't. I'm his father and you can't take that away from me.'

'Nobody is taking anything, Brando. Grow up, for fuck's sake.'

My grandfather emerges, sideways, from the living-room. 'You two all right? Keep it down, the Sprog's asleep.'

'I was just going, Donal.' Caroline is pulling her coat from the coat-stand by the door. 'See you. Okay?'

'Goodnight, Caroline.' He sees her to the door in his slippers, leaving me alone, erect and impotent.

'Oh, Brandon, Brandon,' he says on his return. 'What am I going to do with you?'

'She wants him,' I spit. 'She'll take him away from us.'

He sighs and puts a hand on my arm, leading me towards the kitchen. 'Maybe not,' he says softly. 'But if she wants to, you're making it easy. You know that, don't you?'

'I don't know anything,' I tell him, my frustration spilling over again. 'I don't fucking know anything.'

'Brandon. I don't know what to say to you, boy.' He pities me, barefoot on the linoleum of his kitchen floor with my fists clenched. He stands, comfortable in his slippers, and tries to calm me. 'Tell me what's bothering you, Brandon.'

'I can't, Grandad. I just . . . Oh sweet Christ.' I feel my fingers flex by my sides. A bubble bursts somewhere in my chest and hot tears roll down my cheeks. I am lost. How can anybody understand that? I do not see any future and the present terrifies me. There is no way out. His hand on my arm just makes it worse. No comfort in his comforting. I cannot make it all all right.

'I need to be alone.'

'I love you, boy.' His voice trembles and my tears come fresh. I know. I know he loves me. I know that that should be enough. Him. And Donal. But Christ, Jesus. There should be so much more. I had such high hopes. Is it so unreasonable?

'I need to go to bed.'

He steps back and pats at my shoulders with his wizened

hands. 'Goodnight, Brandon. Sleep well, boy.'

But I will toss and turn tonight. Again. I stand in the bathroom looking at my face in the mirror. An old face. Older than it has a right to be. Sometimes I pause, walking, maybe, with Donal running in front of me, and I am convinced my heart will stop. Broken, it will trickle to a standstill. There are such voids in me, such vacancies.

I say goodnight to my grandfather, leaning around the door. 'I'm sorry. Just . . . Goodnight.

'Will you not stay up? It's early yet. The *Pat Kenny Show* is starting soon.'

He pleads gently. But how can he understand how pathetic I feel in my yellow shirt and grey knitted waistcoat? I put them on for her.

*

I have not told him yet. How can I? I would have to reveal the depth of my lie. And maybe he would tell Caroline and she would take him from me. '*Your Honour, the father's regular source of income is as non-existent as his sanity . . .*'

His holidays have come. At first I left the house at half past nine each morning and stayed away until three. Sometimes I would sit in Redmond Park until it was time to go home or wander aimlessly around the town. On Tuesdays I would queue at the labour exchange in Anne Street. Pay day. And then there is the shopping.

I met Matty Devlin on the main street last week. He looked uncomfortable when he saw me coming but stopped and waited, about to turn up Bride Street. 'Marlowe,' he said when I got closer. 'How're things?'

'No point in complaining, Matty,' I said.

'Aye. No point.' He stood awkwardly, his hands in his

pockets, looking for something to say. His forehead looked sunburned but he had grey pouches beneath his eyes and he was bathed in sweat. He had cigarette ash on his lapel.

'How are the kids?' I asked.

'Obnoxious,' he said, smiling. 'How about Donal?'

'Great. He's great.'

'Good. Good.' Matty glanced up Bride Street, anxious to get away. I decided to put him out of his misery.

'I'm okay, Matty. Really I am. Look, I'll see you around, all right?'

'Yeah. Right. See you. Good luck, Marlowe.' He held his hand out and I shook it. 'Listen,' he said, 'I feel like shite about all this. Give me a ring sometime. I might be able to fix you up with something part-time.'

'Thanks, Matty. I appreciate the thought. You're a good man.'

'Ah fuck,' he said, his face reddening, and he withdrew his hand. I watched him waddle up Bride Street, his rear-end looking like a pin-striped battleship.

Two days later, when I got home from my imaginary job, my grandfather told me that Matty Devlin had dropped dead at midday Mass in Bride Street church. 'It was a massive heart attack,' he said. 'He was dead before he hit the floor. Sure he'll be grand, though. He was a daily communicant.'

*

I cannot link syllables to tell her of the darkness in my soul; yet still we are reliant on the spoken word. If only she could peer into my brain or touch my heart. Communication should be spiritual too.

I do not have the kind of face that gives away that much. Sometimes, when we lived together, amused, I would smile internally. But she would lash out anyway, thinking I had missed the humour in a moment. *'What?'* Baffled, I would broaden my smile until it hurt. *You see?* Too late. The moment would have passed and we would stiffen into cold misunderstanding, Caroline grown bad-humoured and irritable. *'Don't fucking patronise me.'* Ours was a verbal romance, and now I feel that I have left so much unsaid. I am a tongue-tied oaf.

With Rita it was different. She filled the silences with more than words, her body always speaking. There were moments when I felt her vision penetrate my consciousness and my inadequacies seemed to disappear. I was at peace with her, comfortable, knowing that she understood.

I am not a demonstrative man. I hide my feelings deeper than I ought to. When my mother died the centre of my existence altered. I became a man among men, and Francis Marlowe wouldn't raise a pansy. My grandfather tried to compensate but he was ineffective in our syzygy. We orbited each other with cautious unease. My father wasn't one to spare the rod and spoil the child, so I grew wary of him. Thoughts are best concealed and pain is at its most valuable when it is pushed deep and out of sight. He demanded calmness, although my grandfather would have welcomed children's laughter. I often heard them arguing: *'He's still my son. You've already had your chance. He has to learn that life is hard.'* I learned the lesson well.

I do not mean to punish her. Or Donal. It is my fault, my shortcoming. At least I recognise that. I am afraid, but she mistakes my fear for stubbornness. It starts with birthday presents. *I am losing him.* How can I compete? Out of work for months now, the dole can only stretch so far. Is it my ego that prevents a full confession? Repentant, would I come to her, kneeling, if it wasn't for my pride? *I have lied and I cannot support my child.* Would she take pity and protect me?

Would she justify my actions to my son? *It was a white lie. He didn't want to hurt you.* I didn't want to lose him.

She gives him more than I could ever hope to give. The toys. The tenderness. Christ. I have become distant. Detached, like Mother. A foreigner trying to belong. *Needing to belong.* But my need is mistaken for obstinacy and I cannot communicate the frustration that consumes me. I am perceived as hard but inside my heart is breaking. *I am losing him.*

'It makes me look bad,' I tell her, and her eyes cloud over.

'Not now, for Christ's sake, Brando.'

I sulk. It is inevitable. I have grown selfish these past few months. My grandfather excuses himself, disturbed by the shift in atmosphere. Half an hour since the child blew out the candles. Five. My son is five. *I am losing him.*

'So, Donal, are you happy with your presents?' she asks, ignoring me.

'Of course he is,' I snap. From the corner of my eye I can see confusion crossing Donal's face. 'Happy with your presents. Why don't you just ask straight out? Which do you prefer, Donal, my presents or Daddy's? Why don't you just ask what's really on your mind? Who do you prefer, me or Daddy?'

'Stop, Brando. You're being foolish.'

'Am I? Isn't that what this is all about?'

'No. This is all about our son's birthday party.'

'Our son? So now its *our* son? Where were you for all the other birthdays, for all the colds and nightmares and Christmases? Where were you?'

'Bastard.'

'Stop it, stop it.' Donal, screaming, interrupts us. I turn to see him still kneeling at the table, his hands clamped across his ears, tears streaming from his eyes. It is as if the breath has been sucked from me. I feel my chest tighten, my shame amplified by the sudden silence, my son sobbing in the aftermath. My face burns. Caroline moves around the table and crouches beside him, her arms circling him, kisses planted on his wet cheeks.

'There, there, Donal. It's okay. Everything's okay.' I stand apart from them, isolated, my fists clenched, a muscle working in my jaw. 'You had to do it, didn't you? Had to spoil it for him.' Her eyes are hard. I cannot meet them. I watch her hands, instead, gentle on her son's head and shoulders, moving softly over him. Mothering. *Her* son. 'Jesus, Brando. How could you?'

'It's bedtime, Donal,' I say quietly, frightened by my jealousy.

'Brando . . .' She moves to object.

'He's still my son,' I say sharply. 'He lives under my roof. Come on now, Donal. Bedtime.'

The child slides off his chair and brushes past me, sullenly obedient. He turns back to Caroline in the doorway, eyes big and sad. 'I'll be up later to say goodnight,' she says. 'Go on now.' He hesitates; then moves towards the stairs. I start to tidy dishes off the table. 'I don't know what's come over you, Brando,' she says. 'You weren't always like this. You used to be so kind and considerate. So different . . .'

'Everything used to be so different,' I interrupt. 'Life's a bitch and then you marry one . . .'

It just slips out. I cannot help it. My intellect screams at me, pulverises me from the inside. *This is not me. This is not who I am.*

Her face is drawn and white. Her lower lip trembles. 'You fucking bastard,' she says slowly, each word occupying its own space.

'You can't have him, Caroline,' I say calmly. 'I won't allow it. I'll do anything I can to stop you. Anything. I'll . . .'

'You'll what?' she spits, her eyes alive with hatred. 'What will you do, Brando? Big man. What will you fucking do?' Her face is close to mine and I can feel her saliva on my lips.

'Get out of my house.'

She recognises the finality in my words, my tone of voice. An ending. She closes her mouth, more words superfluous, dismissing me. She picks her purse up off the table and walks out of the room without another glance in my direction. I follow her into the hallway, the stiff rigidity of her. Proud. Head high. She does not pause at the front door. This time she leaves in plain view, no sneaking out under the cover of darkness. No notes. She is stronger now. This is her moral victory. *Brando's fault this time. No need for self-recrimination.* She leaves the door swinging open behind her; slamming it would mar the dignity of her retreat. This way she wins. *I close the door.* I force my eyes away from her. Her leave-taking. Oh, Christ. I will not watch her climb into the car. Our eyes will not lock. *I close the door.* I will not apologise. There is no going back. I will not beg. She leaves. Leaves me again. *I close the door.*

Donal watches me from the top of the stairs, our argument still hanging on the house. He is doe-eyed when I turn. His face is dirty from the tears. 'I thought I told you to go to bed,' I say. He flinches at the anger in my voice. He is not used to this.

'Why were you so cruel to Caroline?'

'I wasn't. Now do what you're told. Go to bed.'

'I like Caroline.' He has started down the stairs, defiant. Five years old.

'Donal. Go to bed.' I feel a calmness slip across the fire in my brain. I am left aching and sad, numb now. 'Please.

Just do what you're told and go to bed.'

'But Caroline said that she would come and say goodnight to me.'

'Caroline has gone home, Donal.'

'But I want to say goodnight.' His lip is quivering and I see the tears well up again. He's tired. I know that.

'Go to bed.'

'But . . .'

'No buts. Go.'

'But . . .'

'Donal!' I have never raised my voice to him before and he steps back, tears springing from his eyes again, like tiny pearls that fall across his cheeks. A red mark rises on the left side of his face and it is only when I feel the stinging in my palm that I realise what I have done. By then it is too late.

'I hate you,' he screams at me, then turns and scampers up the stairs. He slams the bedroom door behind him.

My grandfather is standing in the living-room doorway, his glasses on the end of his nose, a paper in his hand. He simply stares at me. I feel my own tears streaming down my face. 'I hit him,' I say, hardly believing it myself. 'Oh Christ. I hit him.'

I start up the stairs, but my grandfather's voice holds me. 'Brandon.' Sharp, filled with urgency. I hesitate on the fifth step. 'Come here, boy. Come here.' He comes to the bottom of the stairs and stands with his hand stretched up to me. 'Leave the Sprog alone. He needs to be alone for a minute.'

'I . . .' But words choke me.

'Brandon,' he coaxes. 'Come here.' Putting an arm around my waist, he pulls me down to sit beside him on the bottom step. 'Relax now, boy. Relax. It happened. You can't change that. Now calm down, boy.'

'I can't believe I hit him.' I force the words through tears.

'Well you did. Now stop feeling sorry for yourself.' His words are hard, matter of fact.

'I swore I'd never touch my child, not after . . .' I feel my grandfather tighten his arm around my waist.

'Hush now, boy,' he says. 'You're not your father. Don't go there. Don't start thinking like that.'

'But . . .'

'Hush now.' I let him pull my head against his shoulder, crying openly now. 'Let it out, boy,' he says softly. 'Let it out.'

But I cannot let it out, not all of it. It is all that I have left. My grief fills me, gives me shape. I have felt something break inside of me, fracture. He will never understand. Caroline will never understand. I feel like Mother, struggling to speak a foreign language, odd words jamming in her windpipe, choking her. Inapt, I become something less . . .

I raise my hand to my son, his hot face flat against my palm, his head snapping away from me, jerking beneath the force of the blow. Flushed, he looks at me, surprised. It takes a moment to register. Thought before the tears come. Before the pain.

My father takes his belt off. I can smell the whiskey on his breath. I can feel the leather across my shoulders before it clears the final loop. Knowing is the worst. Anticipation.

'He's still my son.'

'I hate you.'

I raise my hand to my son . . .

I have become what I hate.

*

That night I have my dream again. Caroline has joined them. They are knotted around the grave, around the child's coffin. Rita's head still rests on Gerald's shoulder. Horst stands, eyes burning. When Gerald looks away from me it is to Caroline. 'I think you are a fool,' he says, glancing back at me distastefully. Horst's words at the airport. A priest, black, opens the coffin and I look inside. The others stare, accusatory. Donal seems asleep, his hands folded across his chest, his hair combed flat. So small. So perfect. I feel that if I shake him he will wake. His lips will split into a grin and he will hold his hands out, wanting me to pick him up, like when he was a baby. Then I see a thin trickle of blood run from his nose and across his upper lip.

'What did you expect?' says Horst, his hand gripping my arm, his voice hostile.

'I don't understand.'

He sneers at me, unmoved by my uncertainty. 'You did this,' he says, and pushes me away from him. 'You killed him.'

My grandfather comes and stands beside me. 'Hush now, boy. You're not your father.' Then Francis Marlowe moves in with his shovel.

REDEMPTION

I

It is like a floodgate opening, memories returning. Gerald, corpulent, regaling me with stories of when he was corset thin. Or Caroline, stretching for my hand while still asleep. The warmth of her beside me, her breath on my cheek. Rita, dark and potent, her strength and her sadness urging me along. The touch of her hand when I feel myself retreating. Her eyes, holding me in place. And Horst, when the wall came down in '89, spilling across the border to the land of milk and honey. Go west, a modern gold rush, chasing after dreams.

*

I put my mouth to the child's, trying to force air into the lungs, his blood drying on my skin. Weeds had already collected in his hair. I pushed his chest with the heel of my hand, trying to kickstart his heart. 'Come on. Breathe, damn you. Come on, Donal.' *Donal? I catch myself. Jason. His name is Jason.* The other three huddled together on the river bank, shivering and turning blue. Blue, like Jason. His skin was clammy to the touch, like rubber, cold from the water.

They had watched me awakening, plunging, urgent, into the river, like a mad thing, stretching for him. Sentinels, they watched me drag his streaming body through the mud and collapse beside him in a wet heap on the grass, my tears mixing with the freezing water in my clothes. No time to think, I angled his head backwards, trying to free air passages, moving his tongue aside. I pinched his nose and blew hard into his lungs, frightened at how cold he felt, the river water pooling in his belly button. I could feel myself shaking, trying to ignore the shock. *He needs me* . . . I closed my fist and thumped his chest. His body jumped and water fountained from his gaping mouth. But his eyes remained glazed, staring blindly at white clouds floating undisturbed above us. I put my cheek to his open mouth, hoping to feel cold breath come faint against my skin. Nothing. I turned my face and blew again, my teeth tapping against his, my fingers tight across his nose. When I hit his chest again I heard a rib snapping like a dry twig underfoot. 'Come on, come on,' I heard myself muttering. 'Live, God damn you.' And then I was shaking him, his head lolling back, my fingers digging into his shoulders. 'Fuck you, fuck you,' I screamed at his sightless eyes. 'You can't die, you can't. Christ. No. Donal.'

I hugged the child to me, his wet hair like soggy sponge against my neck, and rocked back on my heels. I felt my chest tighten, my mouth opening. My eyes burned. Saliva stretched between my lips and I could feel my nose running, hot rivulets escaping me. *Abandon ship.* I could not relieve the aching in my chest. I wanted to scream again, but no sound would come. As if I had given him my breath and, none left for me, I clung to him, all stopped. Breathless.

At last the sob came and I could breathe again. I saw the children reaching for each other's hands. 'What have I done?' I asked them, their faces pale, chins trembling. 'What in Christ's name have I done?' But they just stared back at me, their tears mirroring my own. There was nothing to be said.

*

'Go home,' I tell them, still cradling Jason's lifeless body. They are rooted to the spot. 'Just . . . Go home.'

Peter takes a step towards me. 'Is he dead?'

'Yes.'

Grace wraps her arms around William and buries her head in his shoulder. I can see her trembling. Her blond hair hides her face from me.

'We can't,' says Peter.

'What?'

'Go home. Not now. We're murderers.' His voice is flat, unemotional. I know that he is suffering from shock. He bites down hard on his lower lip, drawing blood unknown to him.

'No. It was an accident. It's okay.'

'But he's dead.'

'Yes.'

'They'll put us in jail.' There is panic lurking close behind his eyes. The others look to him, their leader.

'Or me.' I look straight into his eyes, accomplice, and see him comprehending.

'They can't. You didn't do anything.'

'You're right. I didn't. Nothing. I should . . .' But should-have-done won't change anything.

Grace walks towards me, uncertainly at first. She stops a foot away from me and stretches out a hand, touching Jason's shoulder. 'Jason?' Her brow puckers. She looks at me, her eyes wide. 'I didn't mean . . .'

'It's okay,' I say softly. 'Everything will be okay.' I touch her cheek, look into her dark eyes. *Like Donal's. Christ.*

'It won't,' says Peter, defiant suddenly. I can see his fist balling again. He is struggling not to cry. 'Nothing will be okay. Are you stupid or something? Nothing will be okay.'

'Stop it, Peter.' Grace clamps her hands over her ears

and shouts at him. 'You're frightening me.'

'Well you should be frightened then,' he snaps at her. She stands still and fresh tears tumble silently from her. William hovers in the background, afraid to look at Jason. 'Will you help us?' Peter asks, his eyes pleading.

'Yes.' I have no choice. It is as if my fate was sealed when I followed them from school. Joined then, a part of them. Belonging to them. 'I'll help you.'

'We have to get away from here.'

'I know.' Another bond is formed. *We're all in this together.* Now I am at their centre, recognised. They gather around me. Accepted, I am absorbed by them, assimilated.

'What's your name?' says Grace, her fingers in my beard. Jason, forgotten, is limp in my arms.

'Johnny,' says Peter, 'he's called Johnny.'

'I . . .' But no. I need a new identity. There are echoes that I'm not prepared to face yet. 'Yes. You can call me Johnny.'

I tell them to go home and pack. *Bring warm clothes and talk to no one.*

'What about Jason?' Peter asks.

'Never mind,' I say. 'I'll look after Jason.'

'But where will we go?' asks William, breaking silence. The words seem uncertain in his mouth.

'I know a place,' I tell him. 'Somewhere safe.'

*

I wrap my coat around him and fill the pockets with stones.

You'll need stones in your pockets, or you'll blow away. I picture myself, caught weightless on the bridge at night. Feather. Lifted, like gossamer, I float, ghostly then, on slipstreams high above the town, twin steeples shrinking far below me.

Jason sinks in deep water underneath an overhanging branch. Stones in his pockets, anchors, keep him from floating away.

*

The spare key is where it always is, inside the model windmill on his flowerbed. I wondered on the way here what I would tell him if he were home. How I could explain. What if he is dead? It is not unthinkable, the man is in his eighties. But the house is unchanged, marked by the same small neatness as its owner. Nothing has changed. He still spends his afternoons in the bookies and the pub it seems. I let myself inside.

I come clean in his bathroom, showering in cold water. The immersion is only ever switched on half an hour before his bath. I use his razor. It is a face I know now, even underneath the strips of saliva-soaked toilet paper I use to patch it up. It seems I clean up well, all things considered. My chin looks white, pale, where the beard used to be, compared to the sunburnt rest of me. Nothing that a day or two of stubble won't take care of. There is more grey than I remember, though, dotted through my hair, a testament to living rough.

I see a child's face in the mirror. It is Donal that I drag from the riverbed. My mouth is locked to his and I am blowing futile air into his flooded lungs . . .

I squeeze my eyes shut, exorcising demons. There are things I can't remember. Not yet. Fragments shuffle past, unwelcome. Policemen knocking loud on doors. Sleepless nights spent mourning . . . No. I must resist. I must keep the pain at arm's length. Ignorant, I can survive.

I find my clothes carefully folded in the chest of drawers in my old room. Cleaned. As if he has been waiting for me, prepared for my return. What will I tell him? That I am all right? That I am recovering? Recovered? *It's okay, Grandad, I'm as right as rain.* I drop the towel and step into clean underwear.

Downstairs, I lift the telephone. Jacinta answers on the third ring. When I tell her who it is she is amazed. 'Brandon? Jesus. How are you? Now there's a blast from the past. My God, how long has it been? How have you been keeping?'

I tell her what I need and she says that she can arrange it. She calls me back ten minutes later. 'You're in luck. There's a lorry off to France tonight. He'll meet you in Rosslare at five o'clock.'

'You told him that I'd have the kids with me? You know. EuroDisney and all.'

'Jesus, aren't you very good all the same, though?'

'Aye. Thanks, Jacinta. You're a star.'

Safe passage.

*

He came home at three o'clock, his bets laid, his Guinness settling. I was sitting in the kitchen, waiting, my travel bag packed and ready at my feet. I stood up and coughed as he walked into the room. He jumped, startled. 'Jesus, Mary and Joseph,' he said, his hand clutching at his chest above his heart.

'It's okay, Grandad. It's me.'

'My God, Brandon. You nearly gave me a heart attack. Jesus.' He sat heavily on a chair in the corner, his thin legs folding under him like matchsticks. I moved towards him but he waved me away. 'I'm okay. It's all right.'

'I'm sorry. I didn't mean to frighten you,' I said. 'I wouldn't have waited, but I thought that it would be worse if you came home and thought that you'd been burgled.'

He coughed and looked sideways at me, his expression a mixture of fright, anger and amusement. 'You could have phoned or something. Christ, you gave me the fright of my life.' He laughed when he saw my face drop. 'No. That's stupid. It's okay. I'm glad to see you. I've been worried sick. Where on earth have you been? Are you all right?'

I looked at my shoes. They were shiny, polished by him in my absence, ready for my first steps. A new beginning. 'I'm okay.' *Recovering.*

'You just disappeared.'

'I know.' But the details were still unclear, my memory was coming back selectively, too much to absorb. 'I'm sorry. I just . . . I got lost for a while, Grandad.'

'It's all right, Brandon. I miss him too.'

'Aye.'

'Are you okay, now?' He touched my hand, his fright forgotten. 'Really? Are you back for good?'

'No.' I bit my lip, like Peter at the river. Peter. I closed my eyes and saw Jason, wrapped in my coat, descending to the riverbed, a weedy place. Mud billowed around his head, like mermaid hair, his boyish features looking almost feminine, his eyes still open, staring. I had closed them with a thumb but they flew open when his body hit the water and for a heartbeat I thought that the coldness of the water had revived him, resurrection. I opened my eyes and looked at my grandfather, leaning towards me in his chair. 'I have to go again,' I said. 'I just wanted . . .'

'Talk to me, boy.' He held my hand and looked searchingly at me, concern radiating from him like a beacon.

'I wanted to tell you that, whatever you hear, whatever is said, just . . . Look. Don't believe it. I'm still Brandon Marlowe, still your grandson. I wouldn't . . . I . . . Shit. This isn't making any sense. Just believe in me, okay. I need to know that you believe in me.'

'I always have.' He squeezed my hand.

'I know.'

'What kind of trouble are you in, Brandon?'

'I can't talk about it. Not now.'

He let go of my hand and looked away, pursing his lips. 'Okay. It's up to you, Brandon.' He looked back at me, his eyes clear, free of accusation.

'Thank you.' I wanted him to put his arms around me, to comfort me, like when I was a child and my father would storm from the house, leaving hurt and accusation hanging in his wake. Or like he did with Donal, when he rescued him from nightmares in the dead of night and, in the next room, I would hear his soft voice coax the child to safer sleep.

'Look, Grandad,' I said. 'I have to leave now. I just wanted to see you before . . . That's all.'

He peered around me at my travel bag, abandoned beside my chair. 'Can you tell me where you're going?'

'No. I'm sorry. It's better if I don't.'

'All right. But do you have any money?'

'No. I . . . Can you . . ?'

'Wait.' He stood and walked across the room. The coffee can was still on the shelf above the cooker. He reached inside and pulled out a role of banknotes, tied with a rubber band. They felt crisp and heavy when he handed them to me. 'The rainy day money,' he said. 'Is it raining, Brandon? Can you at least tell me that?'

'Pissing,' I said. 'God bless you, Grandad.' I pocketed his money and put my arms around him. 'I love you, Grandad. You know that, don't you?'

'I know, boy.' His voice came muffled from my shoulder

and when I stood back he leaned against the table, his face set in a hard mask. 'There must be something else,' he said. 'Something I can do. Brandon, we're family. Let me help you. Whatever it is.'

'No. There's nothing.' I put my hand on his shoulder and squeezed, smiling sadly at him, knowing that I could not reassure him. 'Only pray.'

'Sure, don't I do that already. All the time. I storm heaven for you, boy.'

'Well, keep it up.' I hoisted my bag on to my shoulder. 'I have to go now.'

'Wait,' he said, a hand on my arm. 'At least stay for something to eat, a rest. You look awful, Brandon.'

'I can't.' I headed for the door. 'I'll call you if I can, Grandad. I'm sorry. I have to go.'

He followed me to the front door and when I stopped to close the gate I looked back and he was still standing there, his hand resting on the letter box, the stooped shoulders of an old man. Older than he had ever seemed, somehow, and beaten. I raised a hand half-heartedly but he did not acknowledge it. Instead he just stared at me solemnly from beneath the bushiness of his white eyebrows; torn, perhaps, between the need for discretion to pacify my fragile sanity and the need to shake me by the scruff of the neck and compensate for Father once again.

*

I meet them outside the railway station. I have grown accustomed to hiding in plain view. William sits glumly amid the luggage, his fist under his chin, eyes cold as I approach. Peter leans against the wall, hangdog, and Grace, unfazed, is tying up her hair and singing softly. She watches her reflection in the ticket-office window. They do not know me at first, expecting Johnny, reprobate. My appearance confuses them, the clean blue jeans and T-shirt, fresh-shaved face. I dump my bag beside them and look them over. Peter looks jumpy, ready for flight. 'Relax, kid,' I say. 'You didn't say a word to anyone, did you?'

Recognition dawns, a sudden widening of the eyes. 'Johnny?'

'Aye.'

'You look . . . different.'

'Same old Johnny,' I say, winking at him. 'Here.' I hand him a twenty-pound note. 'It's better if you do it. Get the tickets. One adult and three children to Rosslare.'

'Rosslare? It won't take them long to find us there.'

'We won't be there. It's only the beginning.'

'Where are we going?'

'Home,' I say. 'I'm going home.'

He looks at me, doubtful. Wondering, perhaps, if he could pin it on me after all. Or maybe that's just me being unkind. I nod to him and smile, reassuring. 'Go on. Good boy. Go and get the tickets. We'll meet you on the platform.'

The other two have wandered over, curious. Grace stares at me, William at his feet. 'Where did your beard go, Johnny?' she asks.

'It fell off,' I tell her and she giggles.

'Your chin is white,' she says, a finger extended towards my naked face.

'Aye. Come on now. William, get the bags. The train will be here soon.' I lead them to the platform. Grace's hand finds mine along the way and, when I look at her, she smiles up at me, content. I could be their father, taking them to the seaside. William struggles along behind us, weighed down by their bag. I wonder if it's full of picnic, crisps and lemonade.

*

If I stop to think, we're lost . . .

Perhaps she's getting home from work now, puzzled by the silence. Inside, her mother scowls and shakes her head. 'I'll murder them.' The grey hair adds to her severity. 'The dinner's going cold.'

'They're only children.' But she frowns anyway, swinging her handbag over the back of a kitchen chair and slipping off her jacket. It isn't like them to be late.

'It's that Jason Walsh,' she says. 'The little brat.'

And further down the road, I think, Margaret Walsh is likely to be unperturbed. Her son is not renowned for punctuality. Maybe she makes his bed and clears his rubble from the floor. It will be dark before she worries, and even then it's likely to be distant. It's not the first time. He's a rascal. 'I'll tan his hide when he gets home,' his father will proclaim. Yet, a field or two away, her son already sleeps. His skin turns mottled white inside my coat on his new bed. There are stones in his pockets and his eyes see only blackness. His lips are long since blue . . .

If I stop to think, we're lost.

II

I enter his bedroom with my head hanging. He is wound on the bed, wounded, a miserable knot, his face turned to the wall. I sit on the edge of the bed and put a hand on his head. He stiffens under me, reluctant to turn. His misery is my penance.

'Donal?' But he will not turn to me. I drag at his shoulder but he resists and I give in. He sobs, his thumb stuck fast in his mouth, his eyes squeezed shut. 'I didn't mean to hit you, Donal. I was wrong. Forgive me. Please.' But still he does not turn. I feel my heart sink even further, a new level of hollowness. I lean over and kiss the side of his head. 'Goodnight, Donal. I'm sorry. I'll try to make it up to you.' I turn the light off on my way out the door.

My grandfather is waiting outside. 'Is he okay?'

'No. I don't know. Maybe he will talk to you.'

I watch the old man shoulder his way into the room, his soft voice urging my son towards him. He will offer a shoulder to cry on, safe arms to circle him, protection from the darkness. He will listen patiently to soft breathing and anguished words, the boy allowing him to carry out this proxy auscultation. The bond between them will be strengthened. Secrets will be shared. He will guide my child beyond his present purgatory. And outside I will wait, inept. I must rely on him to save my son.

*

Max met us in the café, rising when we entered and shuffling towards us with his hand extended. 'Brandon Marlowe?'

'Yes.' The children looked at me, their faces open, wondering. Another alias? An alibi, perhaps. I ignored their unspoken questions. 'Max, is it?'

'Yeah. Jacinta said I'd know you when I saw you.' He smiled and pumped my hand. 'I remember you from when you used to work for Devlin. You handed out the pay packets every Thursday afternoon. You were a popular man.' He was fifty, maybe, with a large flat face and sparkling blue eyes. His thick brown hair was parted neatly and combed diagonally across his forehead. It seemed somehow at odds with his oil-stained overalls and callused hands. 'Are ye all set?' he asked, his eyes dancing across us. 'It's nearly time to board.'

'Lead on,' I said and bent to retrieve our luggage. 'Come on kids.'

We followed him across the car park to where the trucks were gathered. 'Jacinta tells me you're all off to EuroDisney,' he told me, ushering us towards his truck. 'I'm afraid I can only take you as far as Cherbourg, that's where I'm picking up my load. Sorry I can't take you any further, but the rail service to Paris is pretty good. It should get you there.'

'Cherbourg will be fine,' I said.

He had parked near the freight entrance to the docks. 'All aboard,' he said, unlocking the passenger door from the inside and pushing it open for us. 'It's a bit of a squeeze, but sure it's better than a slap in the face with a wet fish.' The children giggled and climbed up into the cab beside him. When we were all settled he threw the truck into gear and nudged his way into the line of traffic waiting to board the ferry. Our journey had begun.

*

On board I upgrade Max's cabin to a four-berth. 'Are you sure you don't mind sharing?' I ask, but he waves away my protestations. *Sure it's all a big adventure.* 'William and Peter can sleep one-up-one-down,' I tell him as we stow our baggage in the cabin.

Later, in the bar, I buy him a pint, and crisps and Coke for the children. We sit on bar stools watching them pass beer mats back and forth. Grace angles her head back and chews open-mouthed, trying not to guffaw. The others laugh and turn away in mock disgust. William looks to me and shrugs, lifting his hands, palms upward as if to say: what can you do?

'They're grand kids,' says Max, turning towards me and folding his arms on the bar in front of him. He is watching the children. 'They're a credit to you.'

'Thanks.' I look hard into my whiskey glass, avoiding his eye.

'Pity your wife couldn't come, though.' The remark seems motivated by a desire to make pleasant conversation, but I sense the danger nonetheless.

'Aye. It was all a bit last minute.' I offer nothing more.

'Do you mind me asking?' He frowns and sips his Guinness. 'What's this Johnny business all about?'

'It's silly really, a long story,' I smile at him, trying to hide my rising panic. *Calm. Stay calm Brandon.* 'I'm actually their stepfather. Daddy doesn't sit too well with them. You know? And I don't want to take their father's place . . . So we settled on Johnny. Sort of a special name between us. It seemed like a good idea at the time.'

'Jaysus, it is. A great idea,' he says, nodding his head, impressed. 'Fucking brilliant.' I feel relieved to have avoided his doubts so easily and he does not question me further. I am still hiding in plain sight.

I wonder if he is their only suspect when she comes in floods of tears to Wexford Garda Station. Does she tell them about her estranged husband, a soggy handkerchief wound around her fingers, the tip of her nose turned red from rubbing? It's dark and they're not home; he must have taken them. Yes. That's it. That must be it. Does she sit quietly, wondering, her mother's arm around her, while a call is placed to Dublin and a squad car is dispatched to track him down? And when he rises from his lover's bed, the perfect alibi, what do they tell him? How does he react? I fancy that he packs a bag and jumps into his car. While his wife sits waiting patiently for news he speeds through Wicklow in the moonlight. And Margaret Walsh comes, worried, with her husband. It is a busy night. Meeting in the waiting room, perhaps they start to put it all together. Frightened, reluctant, they start to realise that something serious is wrong.

'Go home,' the sergeant tells them, 'we'll handle it from here.'

By now, I think that maybe we're pursued . . .

*

That night Grace wakes up screaming. The cabin pitches and rolls in darkness. I catch her thin wrists in my hands and pull her towards me, comforting her. 'It's all right, child, it's all right.' But the unfamiliarity of my contours seems to add to her hysteria.

'Jason,' she screams, just half-awake. 'Jason is dead. We killed him. William. No . . .'

Max snaps on the light. 'Is she okay?' Peter and William sit up rubbing at their eyes and looking blearily at me hugging their panicked sister.

'She's fine. It's just a nightmare,' I say, clutching her head to my chest and smoothing her golden hair. 'Shush, Gracey, everything's okay, it's just a nightmare. It's okay. It's me. Johnny. I'm here now.' She sobs and puts her arms around my neck. 'It's okay,' I tell the others, 'go on back to sleep.' And they collapse back into weary slumber, calmed by the rolling of the ship and the music of the waves outside the porthole. I take her to my bunk and soothe her back to sleep, her small body curled against me, like Donal in those early days in Ireland, when we used each other's heat to beat the nightmares. I lie awake and hold her, my arm around her shoulders, my free hand still rubbing at her hair. Perhaps she has the same dreams as me. Perhaps the crabs come crawling from her subconscious, too, and feed on Jason's eyes.

'Hush,' I whisper in the darkness of the cabin, the ship rolling and creaking around me. 'It's just a nightmare.' Her breathing is regular and deep now. She has long since drifted back to sleep. It seems that I am talking to myself.

*

While we are waiting to disembark, sat huddled, leaning towards the windscreen, Max lifts a cheek and farts. He looks, startled, at the children. 'Well excuse me,' he says theatrically, the picture of injured innocence. They giggle nervously, unsure of him. But when the smell comes wafting through the cab we all groan and Max rolls down the window. 'Oh Jesus,' he says, his expression pained. 'No more curried rice for me.' He waves a hand beneath his nose, then fans the offensive air towards the open window with both hands, as if he is beating at an invisible enemy. 'Get out and walk, you bastard,' he bellows, and we all collapse in helpless laughter.

'You're disgusting,' Grace says, pushing at his arm with

her tiny fist, her face screwed up, a mixture of laughter and distaste.

'I know,' he says in his flat nasal accent, laughing and pushing gently back at her. 'Lord, it's awful, ain't it.'

He leaves us at the train station, climbing out of the cab to wish us well. He hands French money to the children. *'Have a ride on me at EuroDisney.'* They all smile and thank him politely, party to my duplicity. He shakes hands with me and wishes me well. 'Good luck, Bran . . . Johnny.' He winks and lets go of my hand.

'Thanks, Max. Good luck to you.'

We stand together and watch him drive away, the children waving. We have made it to mainland Europe. Fugitives.

*

We did not take the train. Instead I took them to the tourist office and asked there if it would be possible to put us in contact with someone who would take us to Frankfurt in return for petrol money. A thin teenager behind the counter smirked at my halting French, but looked up his database, his fingers flying over the keyboard. 'No Frankfurt,' he said in English, 'but I can get you a lift to Aachen via Brussels. It is with a Mr Lutz. A German. He leaves tomorrow morning.' I told him that that would be fine and he printed off the telephone number and handed it to me.

Mr Lutz was a travelling salesman with a broken nose and smoker's cough. He picked us up at the motel that we had stayed in overnight. I was sitting in the lobby when he asked for me and I went over and introduced myself.

'Hello. I'm Johnny Marlowe,' I said, holding out my hand.

'Herman Lutz,' he said, transferring his cigarette from his right hand to the corner of his mouth and shaking hands with me. He wore a crumpled blue summer suit and scuffed brown shoes and smelled as if he hadn't showered in a week. His hair was sparse but greasy and he had snot in his moustache. He scowled when I produced the children. 'You didn't say anything about kids on the phone,' he said. 'Shit. You should have said.' But he agreed to take us, provided I paid in advance and the children took the bags on the back seat with them. 'The boot is full,' he said.

He led us to a dusty Volvo in the parking lot and we stood waiting while he brushed cigarette packets and fast-food packaging from the back seat on to the floor. I told the children to buckle their seat belts in the back and climbed into the passenger seat. The ashtray was overflowing and I had to push aside a clutter of maps and sweet papers. 'What did you expect?' he sneered. 'First class?'

On the motorway he told me that, although his company paid his expenses, he took passengers to subsidise his income. 'The bastards don't pay nearly well enough,' he said. 'A man must make a living.' I agreed and looked over my shoulder to ask the children if they were okay. They nodded in the back, sitting quietly, afraid of Lutz. The air was stale and I felt ill and wished that he would open a window.

We stopped for petrol just outside Caen. When Lutz finished filling the car and went inside to pay I told Peter and William to take Grace with them to the toilet. 'Why don't you do it?' Peter said, trying to outstare me.

'Because I'm not her brother,' I said evenly.

His eyes dropped away from mine and his shoulders slumped. 'Come on then,' he said sullenly, taking Grace's hand.

Lutz reappeared and pulled the car over beside the restrooms. He got out, leaned against the car and lit a cigarette. 'What do you do?' he asked.

'I'm a kidnapper,' I said, straight-faced. I didn't like the man.

'All right. Be like that,' he said, and turned his back to me. 'I was only trying to make conversation.'

'I'm going to get food for the children,' I said. 'Can I get you anything?' But he ignored me. I bought a sandwich for him anyway.

When we got to Brussels he told us to wait for him in the centre for an hour, he had a delivery to make. 'It wouldn't do for me to be seen with you,' he said. 'I could lose my job.' His anxiety comforted me. He would be unlikely to come forward with information about us when the story broke. I told him that I would pay him another hundred deutsch-marks when he collected us. I didn't want to be abandoned. The money was running out.

*

I think of Max, picking up a newspaper on his return to Ireland and seeing their pictures on the front page. His jaw dropping, fingers tightening around the printed pages. 'Johnny me bollox,' he will say on his way to the telephone.

*

I called Sheila from a phone box in Brussels. It wasn't her who answered the phone. 'Who's calling?' asked a man's voice, possibly her husband's.

'Bran . . . No. Wait. My name is Moses. Tell her that it's Moses calling.'

'Okay.' He sounded amused. I heard him drop the receiver on a table, his footsteps echoing on tiles. His voice drifting from a distance, calling, 'Sheila, it's for you. Someone called

Moses . . .' The display on the telephone counted down the units on my card. I drummed my fingers and waited, listening for her. At last she broke the silence on the line, sounding winded, as if she had been running.

'Moses? Jesus Christ, how are you? Where are you? Moses, are you there? Hello?' Words came tumbling from her, like circus acrobats, boundless.

'Sheila. Hi.'

'God, Moses. Hello. Where have you been? Where are you?'

'I'm in Belgium, Sheila . . .'

'Belgium? Jesus. What are you doing in Belgium? I can't . . .'

'Sorry, Sheila,' I interrupted, 'I haven't got long. You have to listen. I only have a few units left.'

'Give me your number, I'll call you back.' She sounded businesslike suddenly, the breathless excitement evaporating.

'Tell me about Crunchy,' I said, and there was silence for a moment. I squeezed my eyes shut and gripped the receiver, certain. Knowing. 'He died, didn't he? He's dead.'

'I'm sorry, Moses.' Her voice was soft, subdued. She recognised the need to step gently. 'Truly I am. Are you okay?'

'Yeah. I'm . . . Thank you. Thanks for telling me. I'm glad that I heard it from you.' There was beeping on the line. My time was running out.

'Give me your number, Moses,' Sheila said, her voice full of urgency, as if she was afraid that I would not call back, that if the line was lost she would not find me again. I called the number out to her and she repeated it. 'Hang up,' she said, 'I'll call you right back.' I put the receiver on the hook and waited, looking through the dirty glass at the children standing together in the Grande Place. They looked like any other children, here with tourist parents, pointing at the gold-trimmed architecture, necks craned, thinking of McDonald's. *I imagined Crunchy slipping on the cobblestones, his crutches sliding out from under him. 'For fuck's sake,' he would say, turning towards me, cackling, his teeth black and uneven. He would be amused by the crowds sitting outside restaurants sipping beers. He would move among them, maybe, with his hat. 'What are you doing with them fucking kids, Moses?' he would ask. He would scratch his arse, screw up his face and put his head to one side, an eye piercing me. 'Are you mad or what?' Yes. Mad, Crunchy. That surely must be it.* When the phone rang I jumped. I reached for it and picked it up. The plastic was warm and sticky in my hand. Sunshine beat through the glass of the phone box, making me feel as if I was caught in a searchlight, conspicuous and frightened. I knew what I had to do, knew what I would tell her. I was afraid.

'Moses? Are you there, Moses?' Sheila's voice came tinny through the wires.

'Yeah. Sheila.' I sighed. 'It's me. I'm here.'

'Moses, what the hell are you doing in Belgium?' She sounded on the verge of laughter. She had probably conjured up a mental picture of me, lying in rags on Grafton street, ragamuffin, stale breath and glazed eyes. On holiday now, frightening the locals.

'I . . . It's a long story, Sheila. Look. I don't have time. There are things I have to tell you. I know who I am now. My real name is . . .'

'Brandon. Brandon Marlowe,' she interrupted me. 'Am I right?'

'Yes. I . . .'

'I knew it,' she sounded pleased with herself. 'I found your records in the hospital, but they won't let me have the details without consent. I didn't want to contact your family in case . . . Well anyway, I've been looking for you everywhere. I can't believe you know. I wanted to tell you. Listen, this is great. Tell me, how much do you remember?'

'Enough. Well . . . Nearly everything. But it's not important, Sheila. You must listen to me. Please.' I paused, waiting for my words to sink in, wanting her to realise the profundity of the moment.

'Okay, Moses. Go ahead. I'm listening.' She spoke slowly, as if to a child. Patient. Exaggerated tolerance. *If you say that it's important then I'll play your little game.*

'You're the only one I trust, Sheila. His parents have to know.' I paused again. I could hear her breathing on the line; I could sense her stiffening, the mood change. As if something in my voice was getting through, as if suddenly the gravity of what I was about to tell her had penetrated her consciousness. *No game. These are adult things we're juggling. The stuff that nightmares are made of.* I knew that she was alert then; I had her complete attention. 'They'll find the child . . . I put his body in the river, Sheila, underneath a tree.'

'Jesus Christ.' I heard the receiver clattering, as if, redhot, she had dropped it on the table.

'Sheila? Sheila, talk to me,' I shouted into the telephone. I needed the connection. I needed her to transmit information. There was a scraping sound and then she was back on the line, high-pitched, a scream behind her voice.

'Oh Jesus, Moses. What are you telling me? Why me? Why are you telling me?'

She sounded hysterical. I spoke sternly to her. 'Sheila, stop. Control. Okay? I need you to stay calm. Focus. Listen to what I'm telling you. This is important.'

'Okay.' Her breathing was fast and shallow, words punctuating panicked inhalations. 'I'm here. I'm listening.' She was trying to control herself. I pictured her shivering and wiping fiercely at hot tears, her husband standing close to her, a hand on her arm, concerned, his face a question mark.

'Near the house. They'll find a rope hanging from a tree.' I continued to speak evenly, my voice sounding calm, almost dispassionate. 'And children's things. Some toys they left there. A football . . . Dolls . . .' I thought about their campsite, the days that I spent watching from the bushes. *Jason, hugging himself, his freckled face puckering with laughter.* I forced the thought away. 'Further down the river, just a hundred yards or so, there is a tree that grows out across the water, almost parallel. That's where they'll find him. Do you understand?'

'What have you done?' she moaned, terrified, her voice a hoarse whisper. 'Oh my God. Moses . . . What have you done?'

'It was an accident. I . . .' But how could I explain? How could she understand? My son, Donal, lost to me and now . . . 'His parents need to know.' I closed my eyes and took a deep breath. 'His name is Jason. Jason Walsh. From Wexford. It happened in Wexford. You should call the garda station there. They'll be looking for him.'

'Oh my God. My God. This isn't happening. This isn't true.' I wasn't sure if she was listening anymore. Her voice seemed distant, as if she was sinking into shock.

'Sheila. Listen. Do you understand?'

'Why are you telling me this? Why me?' There was anger in her voice.

'It's not about you, Sheila. The parents need to know.'

'You evil bastard.' Her voice was cold, venomous. 'How could you kill a child? How could anybody . . . ? I trusted you. I tried to help you. How could you?' But her words descended into muffled sobs and sniffles, as if she was stuck between anger and disbelief, expecting to wake up any moment.

'The others are safe,' I said. 'You must say that too. The others are safe.'

'Others?' It was as if she had been slapped. 'Oh Jesus, there are others.' She paused, as if suddenly the pieces fit together. 'You have the Bennett children, don't you, Moses? The ones that disappeared in Wexford. They're with you.'

'Yes.'

'You have to tell me where you are, Moses. Exactly where you are.'

'They're safe. Just tell the parents. Okay?'

'Moses, tell me where you are.'

'I can't . . . Look, they need to find the body. They need to know. It's important that they know. He should be buried. They have to bury Donal.'

'Donal?'

I hesitated, confused, trying to stop the rush of thoughts. I bit my lip. 'My son,' I said, 'Donal is my son.'

'Your son? What does this have to do with your son, Moses? What does this have to do with Donal?'

'Nothing. I . . . Look, tell them. That's all.' I hung up and pushed my way out on to the square. The children came towards me. I heard the phone ring again behind me but I ignored it. I caught Grace's hand and we hurried off through the crowd of sightseers, Peter and William following close behind us.

*

The ambulance took him, took away my child. Then, later, when the dust settled, it came back for me.

III

If I teach him to ride a bicycle, perhaps we can be friends. We have so much in common. Raised by men. I too know what it's like to lose a mother. But his lethargy worries me, keeps me awake at night. The way his eyes become hooded when I walk into the room. My grandfather says he just needs space.

Caroline's absences are more painful than my own. She has taken my hope as well as my son. She has taken everything. Now I pray for dark chills, the onset of my illness. They do not come. Instead I am forced to live with myself, forced to face fundamental demons. I am forced to make amends.

I find a job. Fresh start. A new beginning. I tell him in the evening, when I'm putting him to bed. 'I have a new job, Donal. It means better times. I start tomorrow. Tomorrow we'll start again, okay?' But he remains silent, his back to me. I sigh and stand up, moving across the room. I pause in the doorway. 'Donal, I'm trying. Help me out. Please.' Still silence.

I am closing the door when I hear his voice. 'Daddy?'

'Yes. I'm still here.'

'I'm sorry, Daddy. I love you.'

When I go to him he puts his arms around me. I bury my face in his shoulder. It is as if a wave breaks over me. I weep slow tears into his warm pyjamas.

*

In Aachen, I used the last of my grandfather's money to buy train tickets to Frankfurt. 'You must change in Köln,' the sales assistant told me, a cherry-red scarf around her neck, matching her Deutsche Bundes Bahn badge. She spoke slowly in a loud voice, as if I was deaf, and gestured with her hands, leaning towards me across the desk. She must have heard me speaking English to the children. *Ausländer.* I wanted to tell her that I was not a foreigner, that I was coming home and I belonged here. 'Go to platform number three,' she said in stiff German. I thanked her, gathered up the tickets and walked away.

William asked for a sandwich on the train. 'I'm sorry, I told him. There is no money left.'

Peter told me that I was a fool. 'What were you thinking of?' His eyes were full of fire. 'Taking us here with no money. What will we do now?'

'Rita will look after us,' I told him. 'Soon we'll be with Rita.'

But the child stood up and pushed past me, storming down the aisle, his shoulders knotted with anger and frustration.

*

When I think of him now he is a corpse, thin beneath a sheet. His white arms, folded over him, are bones, no more, no less. His fingers are inanimate, their complexity irrelevant. Funny I should think about his fingers. When he was a baby they fascinated him, moving independently, and pointing. He would lie on his back for hours, studying them, as if they belonged to someone else, hypnotic and puzzling. Now they are splinters, curled against his skin. His palms are placed flat on his pigeon chest, his wrists crossed. It is as if he is sleeping. Eyes closed. I expect to see a ripple in the eyelids, a narrowing of the space between his eyebrows, preparing the next question for Daddy. But Donal is gone. I must remind myself that this is just a corpse.

The train slips sideways on the track and jars me into consciousness.

*

I would have gone straight in, not thinking. I would have walked them to the door. But Peter tugged my sleeve and pointed with his chin to the police car parked around the corner. We walked straight past, eyes front. I could have looked up at her window. Perhaps I would have seen her looking out, her dark hair tied up off her face, policemen flanking her, warning her that I should be considered dangerous. I wonder if they told her that I had already killed a child. Or two. Did she believe them? Maybe, if she had seen me, she would have met my eye and shook her head, almost imperceptibly. *Not safe. Just keep on walking.* Or maybe she would have pointed excitedly in my direction. *There he is, the bastard. Murderer.*

I was shaking when we got on to the tram. 'Two stops,' I told the children. 'That should be enough.' It wouldn't do to be stopped for fare evasion.

*

The burnt-out hut was just inside the edge of the forest. I had remembered it from a walk long ago, the path through the allotments, Donal on his tricycle, Rita's hand in mine. *A barbecue got out of hand. We saw the flames licking at the pitch roof in the distance and I ran along the path and joined a line of partygoers ferrying plastic buckets full of water from the river to the fire. I felt my face grow warm and the rhythmical pull of the*

bucket handles on the palms of my hands. Grimly determined,
we bent our backs and worked together to salvage what we could.
The owner stood black-faced and sombre in the heat, throwing
bucketful after bucketful of water at the orange fireball that had
once been his refuge from Sunday afternoons at home. Later, he
sat among us on the grass and looked at the steaming remnants
of his shack. 'It isn't worth it,' he said to me, his jaw set. 'We
should have let it burn to the ground . . .' But it was home for
us now and I was glad that we had bothered.

I was used to living rough; for me it was no penance. But
the children muttered and complained. 'The floor is black,
Johnny. There are no beds. Where will we sleep?'

I cut leafy branches in the forest, dragged them inside
and covered them with clothes. Furniture of sorts. 'It will
do,' I told them. 'Our hideout. Pretend that it's a game.'

'It's not a game, though,' Peter said, his face fierce. 'Why
have you taken us here?'

'Because it's safe,' I said.

He snorted and turned away from me. Grace was
unpacking, humming to herself. She placed her dolls carefully
on the charred window sill. William had gone outside to
explore. 'Safe?' Peter stared sullenly at me. 'Like Rita? That
safe? What will we eat? How long will we be here?'

'Well . . . Look, I'll contact Rita later.'

'But they already know we're here. They're looking for
us. It isn't safe.'

I looked at my jeans. There were black circles at the knees
where I had knelt on the burnt floor to stretch clothes across
the branches. I was starting to look the part again. I hadn't
shaved in several days. Peter and Grace looked grubby too.
I knew that I must be careful, that they would attract
attention before long. Grace had a black streak across her
face where she had rubbed at a cheek with a filthy hand.

Peter's nose was black. He must have been picking it. I smiled.

'It isn't funny,' he said angrily. 'You're supposed to be helping us.'

I ignored him and walked outside into the sunshine. William was standing by the river, a stone in his hand. He was staring at it, transfixed, and moving his hand around as if testing the weight. I coughed and crouched down beside the doorway. He looked up when he heard me and stared at me, his face dark. I knew that he was thinking about Jason. About how it felt when the rock struck, dousing his anger. He looked at the stone in his hand again, then back at me. He turned and flung the stone as hard as he could into the water. Then he walked past me into the hut, as if I wasn't there.

*

I wonder if her eyes will widen when they tell her my name. Perhaps she will recall our meeting in the car park. Wild man. '*I knew that there was something familiar about him,' she may say. 'Behind the beard and rags . . . He must have been stalking me. I should have known.*'

Or will she just recall our fumbling in the cinema years before? The Abbey, wasn't it? Or perhaps during the brief resurgence of the Capitol. It was the first time that I kissed a girl with garlic breath, its pungency catching me in the back of the throat when our lips locked. I closed my eyes and persevered, sweet sixteen, ignoring jeering coming from the row behind, my classmates. '*Go on ya boy ya . . .*' I remember the softness of her lips and her tongue, hard and wriggling in my mouth.

When I walked her home we stopped on the apex of the

bridge and kissed again. It was a calm night and we looked back across the lights of the town, her head resting on my shoulder. I put my face in her blond hair, feeling the softness of it on my cheek, kissing the curve of her cranium. Happy, my arm around her waist, conscious of the weight of her breast mere fingertips away. *If I touched it would she mind?*

She asked me in for coffee and I stood awkwardly in the hallway with my anorak pulled tight around me, unsure if my erection had subsided. Her mother clucked around us. 'Can I take your coat?' I shook my head and blushed. She must have known.

Later, on her doorstep, I asked if I would see her again. 'Of course,' she said and leaned over to kiss my cheek. Warm light behind her, she became a pliant shadow. My lips found hers again, lingering on the dry softness of her swollen skin. Her hair fell across my shoulder. She leaned against me in her stockinged feet, hanging from the door jamb, her hand against my chest. 'It's late,' she said. 'Go home.' But I got an arm around her and held her tight against me, her breasts soft between us. She pushed herself away from me, laughing, looking back across her shoulder, conscious of her mother in the living-room. 'Go to bed,' she said, tightening her lips and widening her eyes in mock frustration. Then she leaned into me again and kissed me fast and hard. 'Go home,' she giggled through white teeth.

I took a step backwards, kissed the tip of my finger, and touched her on the nose. She smiled and backed into the hallway. I turned and walked down the road, not looking back. *Stay cool, she might be watching.* But when I got around the corner I could not contain the smile. I began to run, jumping up and brushing overhanging leaves with the tips of my fingers, elated. *Yes!*

When I called the next day her mother told me that she

wasn't home. And when I met her on the main street she looked through me, as if she didn't know me, walking past me with her friends. I felt foolish, crushed in her path, like detritus, discarded. I thought my heart was broken.

So when they ask me how I came to be there, I tell them that I used to know their mother. Back when we were young. Friends once, long ago. It does not explain much, and Peter looks at me with thinly veiled suspicion, but William and Grace think that perhaps I am their guardian angel.

*

Horst came shuffling in the streetlights, his trumpet case clutched underneath an arm. I climbed on to the tram a carriage behind him, vigilant, afraid they might be following. I could see his lips moving in the next carriage, his bony fingers tapping out a rhythm on the handrail, running over music in his mind. His Adam's apple bobbed above the open neck of his white shirt, his bow tie hanging loose beneath the collar. When he glanced in my direction I hid my face behind my hand, pretending that I was scratching at my forehead.

He jumped off the tram at Konstablerwache and I followed him along the Zeil, a hundred paces back. I caught up with him at the Hauptwache and put a hand on his shoulder. 'Horst.'

He turned, startled, pulled, perhaps, from a trumpet concerto, *adagio*. His craggy face cracked into a smile when he recognised me and he threw his arms around me. 'Brandon.' He squeezed me and lifted me off the ground, then dropped me and slapped my back. 'What are you doing here? My God.' His smile faded suddenly and he looked around him, remembering. 'The *Polizei* have been to see us,' he said in hushed tones. 'They asked us questions about you.'

'I know. I saw them from the road.'

'Are you in trouble, Brandon?' He put a hand on my shoulder and stared straight into my eyes, his face sombre.

'Yes. I think I am.'

'What can I do?'

His seriousness seemed funny to me somehow. I smiled up into his face. 'Thank you, Horst. You have restored my faith. You know, just because you're paranoid doesn't mean that everybody isn't out to get you.'

He blinked and shook his head, scowling at me. 'What? I don't . . .'

'Never mind,' I said. 'Can we go somewhere and talk?'

'Yes,' he said, 'but first I must call Uwe and tell him that I will not play tonight.'

Later, we found a corner table in a quiet pub. Horst went to the bar and ordered two beers while I waited quietly in the half-dark. I watched cars queue at the traffic lights on the corner, their engines growling restlessly until, released, they sprang forward, their headlights sweeping across the window. Assorted drivers, sequestered in their fast cocoons, raced past, oblivious, their minds in neutral, singing with the radio.

Horst carried the glasses across the room and sat down opposite me. '*Prost!*' His eyes were steady on mine. He was waiting for me to explain. I looked down and saw the wedding ring. He followed my gaze and closed his hand self-consciously, and when I looked up he could not meet my eye.

'She needed a husband,' he said quietly. 'After the funeral, when they took you to the hospital, she stopped believing that it would be you.'

'I see.'

'They would have sent her back to South America.'

'Is that the only reason?'

He looked straight at me again, anger in his eyes. 'You know it's not. You know that I love her, that I have always loved her.'

'It's okay, Horst. Do you want my blessing? If you think you need it, then you have it. She's lucky. That's what I think. You are a good man.'

He glanced sideways at the floor, his cheeks reddening, the tip of his tongue caught between his teeth. When he looked up again his expression had softened, the anger dissipated. 'Thank you,' he said.

'Is she okay?' I asked.

'Yes. I give her everything she needs.'

'I'm glad. I'm happy for the both of you.' He nodded acknowledgement. 'And babies?' I said. 'Have you thought about a family?'

'No. She does not want a child. Not after Donal . . .' He looked away again, embarrassed. 'I'm sorry, Brandon. I didn't mean . . .'

'It's okay. I . . .' But a lump rose in my throat and I couldn't bring myself to talk about it. I drank some beer and blinked hard, trying to stop the burning in my eyes.

'For her, it was as if Donal was her own.' His voice matched the sadness of his face, the drooping flesh beneath his eyes, the deep, rugged creases. 'A gift from God, atonement for her sister. Did you know that?'

'Yes. I think, now, that I must have.'

'She will not allow herself to love like that again. To lose . . .'

He lifted his glass quickly and gulped back the amber liquid, his features guarded. I sat across from him, looking at him, touched by his concern for her, the careful disregard for his own feelings. Neither of us spoke for some time.

'How did it happen?' he asked at last, breaking the silence. His voice was neutral.

'I can't . . . Horst, don't make me talk about it. Please. There are things I can't remember. Things that I don't want to.'

'You have to face it, Brandon,' he said gently.

'That's what they told me in the hospital. But it's not that easy.'

'I know.'

'No Horst. You don't know. Nobody knows.' He flinched at the hardness of my voice but his eyes never budged from mine. 'When the police questioned me, at first they took my silence as an admission of some kind of guilt,' I continued slowly, struggling for some kind of control. 'Everyone convicted me, blamed me, because I somehow blocked it out. I somehow . . . Because I became remote. Horst, I loved him more than anyone. You know that. Rita knows. I could not have hurt him. I . . .' I felt a tear slipping from the corner of my eye. He sat perfectly still, watching me. 'I came home and found him in the bath, my grandfather preparing dinner in the kitchen. He was already . . . I tried to revive him. I put him on the floor and tried to breathe fresh life into my child . . . I tried to start his heart . . .' Horst looked away, out of the window. He bit his lower lip and the moisture in his eyes reflected streetlights.

I thought of my son, cold and lifeless on the bathroom floor, a rag doll. I remembered his chest, the fragile whiteness of it underneath the heel of my hand as I tried to pump life back into him. *One, two* . . . Counting. The desperate breaths I blew into his lungs, his mouth gaping. Repetition, until all I could think about was the counting. Numbers. Until only that made sense. My grandfather's hands on me, pulling me away. *'Too late, Brandon. It's too late. He's gone.'* His tears mixing with mine as we clung to each other, kneeling beside his body on the cold tiles . . .

'It *was* his heart you know,' I said. 'A heart attack. That's what the autopsy said, eventually. Imagine. A heart attack. He was only five years old. Guilt? Sure. It's in my genes. It's my flaw. My mother died when she was forty-one. Another heart attack. And my father was crippled by a stroke. And me? Christ! I'm so fucked up. Of course I'm guilty. Of course I am to blame.'

He reached across the table and took my hand, squeezing it. He said nothing. Horst, of all people, musician, quiet man, knew about the power and the value of silence.

*

I feel him shaking me for work, a grin working its way on to his features. 'Dad? You'll be late. Can't be late for work.' We are friends again. Blood, after all, is thicker than water. We have a history. Five years. I love him and I will have to make it work. We are exploring new beginnings, putting our mistakes behind us. Caroline comes again but not as often. We talked, properly this time, and we agreed: 'We must try to be adult. For Donal's sake.'

I am beginning to feel hope again.

*

'Rita will want to see you,' Horst says. 'Come home with me. She'll be there.' I raise an eyebrow, afraid to ask. He shakes his head. 'She doesn't do that kind of work anymore,' he says quietly, his face expressionless. 'I had my conditions too.'

'I can't go there,' I tell him. 'They might be watching.'
'Who?' he asks. 'Why?'

'Just trust me, Horst. Please. I'll explain it all in time.'

Horst shrugs his shoulders and nods, as if my paranoia is normal. *None of my business anyway.* 'What can I do, then?' he asks.

'I'm sorry to ask, Horst, but I need money. For food.'

'Of course,' he says. 'But everything is closed. We can eat here.'

'No. Thank you. I have to go, Horst. I have to get back to the others.'

'Others?' He raises an eyebrow.

'I'm not travelling alone,' I say. 'The others are waiting for me.' He nods, troubled, knowing that I will tell him in my own time. 'I need to talk to you again, and to Rita. Can we meet tomorrow?'

'Yes. I'll talk to Rita. Call us later.'

'I can't. They might have your phone bugged.'

He is starting to look irritated, as if I have used up all his patience. 'Then what do you want me to do?' he asks.

'Meet me tomorrow morning at Römerplatz. Nine o'clock. We'll be there, by the river. But you must be careful, make sure that nobody follows you.'

'Okay.' He nods, but I can see the doubt creeping into his eyes. 'We'll be there.'

Outside he hugs me again, his thin arms strong around my shoulders. He looks worried when he pulls away. 'Come home with me, Brandon,' he says again. 'I'm sure it's safe. Rita will be angry if you don't.'

I smile, backing away from him. 'No, Horst. I can't. Believe me. I'll talk to you tomorrow. Goodnight.' I turn and walk away from him, looking back before I turn the corner. He is still standing outside the pub, his trumpet case hanging loosely from his hand, his head on one side, pensive. I'm sure he thinks I must be mad. I would not disagree.

*

'We are learning,' I tell her, my hand finding hers. Our son walks
ahead of us, a broken branch trailing behind him on the forest
road. She is okay with it, does not withdraw her hand. Instead
she squeezes mine and leans against my arm. The leaves have
begun to change and it is muddy underfoot. Donal wears green
wellingtons. Caroline is all in denim.

'I like your jacket,' I say to her.

'You should,' she laughs, 'you bought it for me. Remember?'

I step away from her and look. 'Oh yeah. In Mannheim. Before
we found out that you were pregnant.'

'Yeah.'

There is an easiness about us, a vague contentment. As if, all
along, all I needed to do was to accept things as they were.

'Remember in Germany,' she asks me, out of the blue. 'The
time we saw the fire hydrant in the forest? Bright red against
the snow when we were walking. "Prepared for forest fires," you
said, laughing. "Trust the Germans." And you couldn't resist it.
You peed on it, standing on one foot while I fell around the place
laughing. You had your back to me and you looked at me over
your shoulder, grinning, urine cutting curves in the snow. "Ain't
I the dirty dog," you said and winked. I could not have loved you
more than I did that day. I know it sounds clichéd but I loved
you then because of how you made me laugh.'

Donal turns and looks at us from underneath his baseball
cap. 'Hurry up,' he says impatiently. It seems that we are
dawdling. The boy is anxious to see what is around the next
bend.

*

209

That night I thought of Rita. I turned, low on my makeshift bed, and watched clouds scud across the sky. The children were dark shadows in the moonlight, their breathing soft and easy.

When I closed my eyes I saw her entering my room, come to comfort me. She let the bathrobe fall and climbed into my bed and put her arms around me. Her lips were soft and moist on my face. I leaned against her for a moment, feeling the warmth of her body against me, remembering her tenderness. I thought that I might cry then but my eyes remained dry. 'I need to be alone,' I said. I felt her nodding in the darkness. She sat on the edge of the bed and I saw her silhouetted against the window, her small breasts firm and erect in the pale blue light, her chin high, proud. I almost reached out to touch her back, to feel her soft skin, warm beneath my fingertips.

'If you need me . . .' she whispered, and I nodded, knowing that she could not see me. She gathered the bathrobe from the floor, stood up and dressed quietly. She leaned over and kissed my forehead before she left. When the door closed after her I knew that I would not sleep that night, that I would think of her lying awake in the next room and Donal lying lifeless in the graveyard.

*

Grandfather blames himself. I can see it in his eyes. I know because I recognise it from the mirror. 'You could not have known,' I say, my arm around him in the churchyard. Caroline hovers in the background. We are not speaking any longer, as if the bond between us has ended with our son and alternatives cannot be endured. I will not lean on her, nor her on me.

She goes to Horst and Rita and I see them shake her hand,

Horst stooped, his long back bending as if he feels the weight of this as well. They will stay with us tonight. One of them will sleep in Donal's bed.

*

I awoke before dawn and in the darkness, for a moment, I forgot. But there was no escape, not any more. I sat up and looked across the room, my eyes growing accustomed to the pre-dawn blackness. I could just make them out, the children, Grace, asleep between her two brothers, how they naturally protected her. I was touched by their apparent innocence. How, unconscious, they seemed like any other children.

But when I thought about the details of what had occurred, of Jason's face sliding pale into the river, his dead eyes staring into mine, I was appalled. It was an accident, I told myself, but then I thought about William swinging the rock, the intensity about them, rejecting Jason's warnings, and Peter's hands, vanished in the cauldron. I thought about Grace, her tiny frame on the river bank, how she looked into Peter's eyes and, when he pushed the boy beneath the surface, how she didn't look away. How their eyes stayed fixed on each other until Jason stopped struggling.

I shivered in the darkness and wrapped my arms around myself. There were decisions to be made but I wasn't sure if I was strong enough to make them. I had crumbled in the past. I had buried my child, buried Donal. *Rita. Rita would surely know what I should do.*

I stood up quietly and moved to the window, peering through the broken frame into the forest. About an hour to dawn, I thought, my hand rubbing at the stubble on my chin. I crouched and stayed like that for a long time, silent, thinking, scanning the undergrowth. The children slept behind me, turning occasionally, limbs twisting, then settling again.

*

At the graveside I think of Jimmy Roche and his severed arm. How he looked at me, uncertain, as I urged him to leap across the track. The fear in his eyes. It was as if we were alone, our eyes locked and me insistent, the train coming fast and furious behind me. Come on, Jimmy, jump . . . And when they lower the casket I look for my father, forgetting for a moment that he is buried close to here. I expect to see his lopsided grin emerging from the crowd. 'Life, son,' he might say, a cigarette hanging from his mouth, ash settling on his pot belly, 'that's what this is. A real bitch, ain't it?' If he were here he would cough and spit and shovel dirt into his grandson's grave.

IV

I panic when the sun comes up, time to be moving, they must be close to us by now. Caroline has told them where I'm going, that's why they've questioned Horst and Rita. I shake Grace, my eyes finding hers, telling her to call the others. *'You must be quiet.'* Whisper. *'Wake the boys. We have to go.'* She nods and when she looks at me they could be Donal's eyes. I almost ask her if she sees the shadows too. Lurking. They join me by the window and I feel Grace's hand worm its way into mine. When I look at her, her face is angled towards me, questioning. *'They'll be here soon,'* I tell her. *'Better move.'*

I carry her from the campsite, the boys following close behind me, like wing men. They are frightened. It seems my panic is contagious. *'Speed,'* I tell them. *'Speed is of the essence. They are close.'*

*

I kissed him when I left for work that morning. He curled away from me in his bed, his eyes tight shut, his fingers spread against his cheek, the wrist bent back. 'Give your old man a kiss goodbye,' I said, smiling and leaning over him again. 'Come on, you lazy fecker.' He muttered, protesting, but opened an eye and looked at me. I gazed into its fuzzy brown, watching the pupil widen, and told him that I loved him. He grunted and turned back to sleep. Then his voice came muffled from his pillow. 'I love you too, Daddy.' At least that's how I remember it.

Francis Marlowe keeps pace with me, dragging his bad leg behind him. He is bent and twisted, like a vicious gargoyle. I can hear him cackling as I carry the child along. Grace. I must remind myself. *I am not carrying Donal downstairs, he is not dripping in my arms.*

'There was always something wrong with you,' my father sneers, struggling to keep up, like Peter and William.

'Shut up,' I snarl, and Grace's head comes round, frightened. She thinks I am talking to her. 'Leave me alone,' I say, ignoring her. 'Bastard!'

'Johnny, you're going too fast,' says William.

'Speed,' I say. 'It's all about speed. Keep up.'

My father sniggers at my shoulder. 'As if it matters,' he says. 'As if you could escape. You can't run. You should at least know that by now.'

I hurry on. Hurry on to Rita. Rita will know what to do.

*

Caroline slaps me hard across the face, then pounds against my chest. 'I should have taken him, like Mother said,' she says, her voice loose, becoming unhinged. 'You irresponsible bastard. How could you let this happen?' I look at her and say nothing. Mourners shuffle uneasily with sandwiches and tea, backlit by bay windows in my grandfather's house, like actors in some tragedy. Horst comes and takes her by the arm. 'No,' she says, pulling away from him. 'No. Take your hands off me. My child is dead.'

'He was my child too,' I want to scream. 'More mine than yours.' But instead I remain silent. Rita watches me from across the room, where she stands with a hand on my grandfather's elbow. She is concerned for both of us. It is as if his age has finally

caught up on him, teasing for so long, finally it has chosen to pounce. He seems small to me, and grey, beside her dark loveliness.

Caroline is crying, her head against Horst's shoulder, her eyes still accusatory. I feel myself slipping, on a knife-edge, like butter, I am slithering away. Rita tries to hold me with her eyes. I see her head shake, almost imperceptibly. But there is refuge from the pain in there, almost prenatal. I can feel myself receding. 'We are mindful of your loss, sir. But questions must be asked.' There is safety there. The walls come up. I feel the teacup slipping from my hand, hear it shattering, see faces turning towards me. Rita comes and holds my hand, she tries to haul me back. No more . . .

I am aware of the blue light flashing when they strap me to the gurney and I leave it all behind.

*

I am becoming Moses again. People slide away from me, alarmed when they see me approaching. Striding, purposeful, and talking to myself. I know what they must think. But now I bear a child, a sacrifice. It makes me visible. She lies limp in my arms, her hands clasped behind my neck, her head against my shoulder. The boys come, trailing in my wake. Grubby, like me. We are attracting attention.

I stand on the tram, the boys beside me, glaring, daring anyone to meet my eye. A ticket inspector gets on and moves through the aisle, but when he gets to me he just walks past, afraid of confrontation. I must look ferocious.

We arrive early at Römerplatz, and wait beside the river. I give Peter some of Horst's money and tell him to go and get some bread rolls in the bakery.

'They won't understand me,' he says sullenly,' 'I don't speak German.'

'So? Point,' I say and look away from him, the discussion over.

William waits with me. He sits beside me on a low wall beside the river Main. Grace is sleeping on my lap, her mouth open, dribbling on to my T-shirt. He leans against me and I feel his arm go around me. 'Thank you, Johnny,' he says, looking up at me. 'Thank you for helping me.' He rests his head against me and I see his shoulders rocking. He is crying.

When Peter gets back with the food I shake Grace, carefully nudging her to wakefulness. They are ravenous. I sit amongst them watching, my appetite abandoned. I am thinking of Gerald now, coming to make breakfast for me and bantering with Donal. *How do you like your eggs?* It seems so long ago, the child happy in his highchair, awash with love.

I see them coming in the distance, along the riverbank. They are hand-in-hand, like lovers, him tall and gangly, her dark and elegant beside him. When they draw near he releases her, her hand falling away from his, as if in deference to my presence. A previous privilege. Her eyes trace the presence of the children, absorbing each of them in turn. At last she looks at me and I stand, lowering Grace gently to her feet on the path beside me. She stands holding my hand, looking at Rita.

'Brandon,' says Rita, her voice cautious. 'Are you okay?'

'No. No I'm not, Rita. I . . . I need your help.' Horst looks at the ground behind her.

She stretches a hand out and touches my face, runs her palm across the bristle on my jaw, her eyes soft, swimming in pity for me. 'Oh Brandon,' she says.

Grace tugs at my arm and I look down at her, look into her eyes. I think of Donal. Remember Donal lying in the bathtub. I blink. Returning. 'This is Grace,' I say to Rita, and then I point to the boys with my chin. 'And Peter and William. I need you to look after them.'

'Tell me, Brandon,' she says. 'Tell me what happened. Tell me what's going on. I want to hear it from you.'

'No time,' I say. 'They will be here soon. They will take me away. You must promise me that you will help the children.'

'Brandon, tell me. Please.' Her voice is calm, insistent. I am soothed by her stillness, her quiet confidence. Mother. 'Explain it all to me.' *I see her lying in my bed, her arm around Donal, smiling at me. 'Our son.'* I put Grace's hand in Rita's, folding their fingers together.

'You must tell them that it was an accident,' I say, starting to move away from them.

'Brandon, wait.' There is an urgency about her. 'You must wait . . .'

Horst is shuffling behind her, afraid to meet my eye. He has a hand on each of the boys' shoulders. I stare at him, suddenly alarmed. 'Horst?'

He looks at me, uncomfortable, and shakes his head. 'I'm sorry.'

'Mummy,' I hear Grace shouting, and when I follow her gaze I see Susan Bennett emerging from an unmarked car, her husband already standing stern-faced on the pavement, his hand resting on the open door. Then Caroline climbs out and stands beside them, her dark hair tied back. She is wearing her funeral clothes.

When I look back at Rita she is reaching for me, pain written all across her face. I pull away. 'Brandon. Brandon, please.'

'You told them,' I say, an accusation.

'I had to, Brandon. They said that you were dangerous. They said . . . They said they wouldn't hurt you if . . .'

'Fuck what they said,' I shout at her. 'I trusted you.'

'I'm sorry, Brandon. I . . . I had no choice.' Tears are streaming from the softness of her eyes.

A man close to us lifts a walkie-talkie and mutters something. Uniformed policemen come streaming from the side streets, running towards me with their guns flapping from their belts like miniature wings. As if in slow motion, I see the hands reaching for me, a host of angry faces.

I am spinning then and running from them, through them, bowling them over. I feel a fist crunch into the side of my face but my momentum carries me on. My elbow catches my aggressor in the midriff and knocks the air from him. He doubles over on the ground behind me, his companions leaping over him. I find myself on the bridge, clear, my feet pounding on the pavement. *You'll need stones in your pockets, or you'll blow away* . . . But they are waiting on the far side, coming towards me, faces set, determined. *Stones* . . . I hear them shouting behind me. I am almost at the apex. A gun cracks. Just a warning shot. Perhaps he will be reprimanded later by his superior. *What on earth were you thinking? Discharging a firearm . . . For what? We had him cornered . . .*

I pause, my heart beating loud in my ears. The river Main is rushing underneath and the wind is tearing at my clothes. They are closing in. Slowing now, knowing that I have nowhere to go. *Murderer. He killed a child.* I look around me, see the hatred in their eyes. I see their fists clenched, I know that they are looking for excuses. *We had no option, sir. We had to beat the living shite out of him* . . . Perhaps if I were one of them I would feel the same. *It was an accident . . .*

I remember him, his cracked teeth and whiskey eyes, the spittle in his beard. I remember willing him to jump. The crowd screaming. 'Get down out of that you gobshite . . .' When I saw the demons raging underneath his skin, I knew he would do it. I knew that he would take the step. I mistook his rage for desperation, his babbling for desperate cries of help.

I climb on to the bulwark, my fingers stretching for the lamp-post . . .

He toppled forward in silence, his arms outstretched, the bottle still clutched in his right hand . . . I wanted him to jump.

There are voices raised. All eyes on me. Policemen form a cordon. Trained. *Nobody make any sudden moves.* Cars, travelling in both directions, squeal to a halt. Passengers leak out on to the road, craning their necks in an attempt to see what's going on. I find it hard to hear above the din.

If it takes a man a week to walk a fortnight . . .

I see Rita come hurrying across the bridge, her eyes attempting to hold me again, urging me to stay. 'Go home, woman,' I would say if she was closer, if this was just between us. 'Go home with your husband and forget me.' Horst runs behind her, his face filled with anguish. When they get to the edge of the crowd of policemen he passes her and tries to push an opening, but they lock arms and bar his way. I can see his mouth moving, he is shouting. *'Brandon. Brandon.'*

Donal's voice coming softly from across his room. 'I'm sorry, Daddy. I love you.'

Caroline finds her way to Rita's side and they put their arms around each other. I can see Rita, tear-strewn, explaining. *'I should not have told them. I should have trusted him.'* And Caroline, consoling. *'But you know you had no choice.'*

They are all here now as I balance on the edge. Gerald and Crunchy stand below me, beckoning, as if they are walking on the water. Crunchy looks solid, standing on his own two feet, his crutches raised above his head, triumphant. 'Come on, you fucker,' he shouts above the rushing in my ears. Gerald shakes his head and smiles at me, his ponytail swinging in the wind. As if to say, 'Another beastly Irishman.'

I look to Rita and our eyes meet. It is as if she sees the change in me, decision. She steps away from Caroline and stretches out her arms to me, her eyes pleading.

My father and mother are standing just behind the others, their arms linked. He is fresh scrubbed and his hair is slicked back. She is radiant. They look young and happy, as if life has not yet had the chance to disappoint them. I think of her parents lying down beside the Elbe.

The children are there, safe with their parents. Acquitted. Grace sits in her father's arms, his hand splayed against her back, her hair falling across his fingers. She is twisting around to look at me and he tries to make her look away. Peter stands apart. Tall. He looks like his father. William holds his mother's hand and cries.

I put stones in his pockets to keep him from floating away . . .

My eyes find Rita again, and she seems small and distant, somehow. 'I love you,' I shout across the crowd. 'I should have chosen you. You know that, don't you? I should have chosen you.' Caroline throws dagger looks, but it hardly matters now.

I think of my grandfather, surrounded by the neatness of his house. Will he cry when they tell him? Will Caroline be the one to bring the news to him? He has outlived three generations. Son, grandson and great-grandson, all gone. Perhaps he will sit, withered, in his chair and then succumb.

I feel my body turning, knowing they will lunge for me, too late. A glove may touch my ankle as I topple, heading waterward, but nothing can stop me now. I feel my fingers slipping on the lamp-post.

They never found the body.

It will come like an old friend. Another absence. Permanent.

Before I hit the water my head clears. I am peaceful.

And in my clarity there is one thought only. Nothing else. Donal. Donal's smile. Together we are happy.